HIS TO OWN

MAFIA KINGPINS
BOOK ONE

AVA GRAY

ALSO BY AVA GRAY

CONTEMPORARY ROMANCE

Mafia Kingpins Series

His to Own

Harem Hearts Series

3 SEAL Daddies for Christmas

Small Town Sparks

The Billionaire Mafia Series

Knocked Up by the Mafia

Stolen by the Mafia

Claimed by the Mafia

Arranged by the Mafia

Charmed by the Mafia

Alpha Billionaire Series

Secret Baby with Brother's Best Friend

Just Pretending

Loving The One I Should Hate

Billionaire and the Barista

Coming Home

Doctor Daddy

Baby Surprise

A Fake Fiancée for Christmas

Hot Mess

Love to Hate You - The Beckett Billionaires

Just Another Chance - The Beckett Billionaires

Valentine's Day Proposal

The Wrong Choice - Difficult Choices

The Right Choice - Difficult Choices

SEALed by a Kiss

The Boss's Unexpected Surprise

Twins for the Playboy

When We Meet Again

The Rules We Break

Secret Baby with my Boss's Brother

Frosty Beginnings

Silver Fox Billionaire

Playing with Trouble Series:

Chasing What's Mine

Claiming What's Mine

Protecting What's Mine

Saving What's Mine

The Beckett Billionaires Series:

Love to Hate You

Just Another Chance

Standalone's:

Ruthless Love

The Best Friend Affair

PARANORMAL ROMANCE

Maple Lake Shifters Series:

Omega Vanished

Omega Exiled

Omega Coveted

Omega Bonded

Everton Falls Mated Love Series:

The Alpha's Mate

The Wolf's Wild Mate

Saving His Mate

Fighting For His Mate

Dragons of Las Vegas Series:

Thin Ice

Silver Lining

A Spark in the Dark

Fire & Ice

Dragons of Las Vegas Boxed Set (The Complete Series)

Standalone's:

Fiery Kiss

Wild Fate

BLURB

He's supposed to marry her older sister, but he can't stay away...

MICELI

The mafia world is cold and cruel. I live by one rule - cut their throat before they cut yours. It's what keeps me ruthless and on top of my mafia family.

But when I see something I like, I take it. It's no different with Alessia DeLuca, who's supposed to marry my rival... while I'm marrying her older sister.

When Alessia sees something she shouldn't, kidnapping her is the only logical answer...

Taking her cherry sure isn't.

ALESSIA

Ever since I met him in a mix-up, I've been intrigued by Miceli Rossi. He says he always gets what he wants, and it's obvious he's obsessed with one thing only... me.

He can force me to marry him. He can even force me to wear his ring.

But I'll make sure I'm the worst wife he could have.

Anything to make sure he doesn't realize how much I want him.

His to Own is book one of the Mafia Kingpins series. This is a full-length standalone novel with these tropes: age gap, mafia, V-card, surprise pregnancy. Guaranteed happy ending!

1

ALESSIA

I've never been so nervous in all of my twenty-four years. Pacing across the room again, I feel like a record on repeat, unable to stop, spinning aimlessly. At this point, I know I must be wearing a trail in the carpet, and I finally pause and wring my hands. My older sister Gia—older by two years—doesn't look even a fraction as anxious as me.

A quick glance at the clock reveals it's only a couple of minutes until eleven.

"How can you be so calm?" I ask in complete exasperation. I feel like I'm on the verge of imploding and she looks so serene and poised. "I'm about to pass out or poo my pants. And you look like you're about to take tea on the lido deck, for God's sake."

She snorts back a laugh. "Because, sis, there's no point in getting worked up. Our fate has already been decided." Gia flips her long, dark hair over a shoulder and sends me a perfect smile. And it is flawless. Everything about Gia is—from her slender figure to her high cheekbones to her polished and refined manners. She should've been a model. Or, the queen of some faraway country. I swear, sometimes I wonder if she sweats or burps or ever feels like she's going to poo her pants like me? She's a classic beauty and always appears so in control. Even when she's not.

Me, on the other hand? I'm a hot mess. I worry, I stress and I obsess. That, of course, leads to the sugar cravings that I can't seem to control. Grabbing another piece of candy from the small bowl on my nightstand, I unwrap the watermelon deliciousness and pop it into my mouth, sucking until my cheeks cave.

"But we're about to meet the men we're going to marry," I say with a frown. "Men we've never met. Doesn't that...I don't know! Bother you?"

Gia sighs in that worldly way of hers. "What do you need to know? They're both extremely handsome and powerful. An alliance between our family and both of theirs will secure the DeLuca name and increase our importance in this city."

Something I care very little about, but I don't say that. My father, Aldo DeLuca, is an important figure in New York City's Italian mafia. Although, he's not quite as powerful as The Rossi or Bianche family. That's why he's planning on marrying me off to Rocco Bianche and Gia to Miceli Rossi.

My stomach turns when I think about the stranger I'm about to go downstairs and meet. A man I'm just supposed to say "hello" to and then "I do" without any time or hope of getting to know him.

He's a stranger! I want to scream. This is so old-fashioned and ridiculous. Or, am I the one who's overreacting? Gia is quite content to marry Miceli and she's never laid eyes on the man. But, she's already had a serious boyfriend and been intimate with someone before. Maybe that's why this isn't as big of a deal for her as it is for me. I've never been in love much less had a relationship and sex or explored any of that. God, I feel like such a baby. A naive little girl. Because the truth is it's more than just sex I've been missing out on. The truth is, I've never even been properly kissed by a man. I mean, sure, there were a few quick pecks here or there when I was in school over in Italy. But those were with boys who I met in town and saw a movie with. Now, I'm dealing with an experienced man who's going to have expectations and desires. How in the world am I ever going to please him?

Biting my lip, my frown deepens. This is awful.

"Stop scowling like that," Gia comments. "Or you're going to make your wrinkles look deeper."

My head snaps up. "I have wrinkles?" I march over to the mirror and examine my face with a critical eye. Well, of course, I have frown lines between my brows. Doesn't everyone?

"Yes, Lessi, and the way you're always worrying, you're going to look like an old lady in a few years if you keep it up." She stands and stretches. "That's why I don't let anything bother me and use so many face creams."

Smoothing my index finger over the deep groove between my eyebrows, I try to flatten the lines. I certainly don't want to look older than my twenty-four years. Maybe I'm going to need to snag one of my sister's many lotions or potions. She's in the know about all of the latest when it comes to looking younger and having gorgeous skin. And hers absolutely glows.

"Well, I suppose it's time to meet my fiancé," she says without a trace of emotion.

My heart rate kicks up and I start wringing my hands again.

Gia walks over and squeezes my arm. "You look like you're about to puke, Lessi. Relax. Why are you so worried, anyway? Just go down-stairs and talk to the good-looking man for a little bit. Be agreeable, smile and laugh at his jokes. Easy, right?"

Easy for her maybe, but not for me. "Yeah, okay," I mumble. Watching Gia whirl away without a care in the world makes me green with envy. I wish I could be more like my sister. But we're pretty much opposites in every way. While she's tall and slender, I'm short and curvy. She's calm and easygoing, I'm anxious and high strung. And, she's a social butterfly. The boys at school all loved and chased her everywhere, while I preferred to stay in my dorm and spend a quiet evening reading or studying.

Well, Gia used to be a social butterfly. Now, she seems so lost and melancholy all of the time. I guess that's what happens after a man breaks your heart. Guess I really wouldn't know.

Maybe I'm just wound too tight and being with Rocco Bianche will help loosen me up and help me learn to enjoy life more. But, for whatever reason, something about him doesn't feel right. Clasping a hand over my stomach, I wonder if I'm going to be sick. *Stop being so dramatic*, I scold myself. *Get it together and go down and meet your fiancé.*

Grabbing another piece of candy, I unwrap it and pop it into my mouth. I don't know why sucking on sweets calms me down—at least a little—but I pause and grab a handful of the candy, tucking them into my pocket. Better to be safe than sorry. Because I have a feeling I'm going to need every single one of them when I go face my husband-to-be...a complete and total stranger, as of this very moment.

Oh, God, help me.

Walking out of the safety and comfort of my bedroom, I head over to the back staircase which will take me down to the library where Rocco is waiting. As I walk down the steps, I wonder if I should've dressed up more or put some extra makeup on? Gia looks like she just stepped off a runway and I look...well, like I always do. I didn't put any extra effort into my appearance and I wonder if that's because a part of me doesn't want Rocco to find me attractive? Because, secretly, I want him to tell my father he isn't interested in marrying me.

Hmm. A devious, little plan begins to form in my brain. Maybe I should purposely try to turn him off. Do something unlady-like or be quiet and mousy, refusing to make polite conversation. Or…maybe I could tell him I'm in love with someone else. Make up a boyfriend and pretend I can't get married because I love someone else and I'll die without him.

No, that won't work. He would probably just get annoyed and then go ask my father about this mysterious stranger, and my clueless dad would quickly deny the existence of my fictional man.

Standing right outside the library now, I hesitate, needing a moment to get myself together. Pushing my nerves down, I force myself to unclasp my hands and let them hang at my sides. I give them a quick shake, hoping to eliminate some of these godawful nerves. Then, I pull in a deep, steadying breath and walk through the doorway.

A very tall man stands in front of the windows, his back to me, and he's looking out over Central Park. His very broad back with wide, muscular shoulders visible through his suit jacket tenses the moment he hears my soft footsteps on the carpet. The first thing I notice is the sharp cut of his lightly-stubbled jawline as turns and, when he's fully facing me, my heart thumps harder. Holy hell, the man is insanely good-looking. I didn't expect to be face to face with a Greek adonis and I suck in a sharp breath.

With a naturally tanned complexion and thick, dark brown, slightly wavy hair slicked back off his gorgeous face, he makes me grab onto a nearby chair for support. Eyes darker than the deepest espresso focus on me and, maybe I'm imagining it, but I think I see approval flash within their depths. And maybe a wave of relief, too.

The other thing I immediately notice about him is he exudes power. It simply ripples of of his firm body in waves. And it has nothing to do with his perfectly-tailored black suit. It's the way he carries himself and the purposeful way he walks toward me. His vibe screams "I'm in charge" and you better listen to every word that comes out of my mouth.

Which, by the way, is a beautiful mouth. His lips look soft, very kissable, and the dark stubble gives him a dangerous look. It also makes me want to reach out and lay a hand against his cheek so I can feel its rough texture. The boys I've known were exactly that—boys with clean-shaven faces. This is a man in every sense of the word and when he extends a large hand, I glance down at it, suddenly at a loss and forgetting basic manners. I'm too fascinated by the groove that appears on his left cheek when he gives me a small smile. A freaking dimple that makes my stomach flip because it's the only thing about him that looks slightly boyish.

"It's nice to meet you," he says, voice so deep I can feel it rumble through my chest and roll all the way down, down, down to my toes.

"You, too," I force out as his huge hand encompasses mine like a softball mitt. Our gazes lock and I stare into eyes that are so dark brown they're almost black. Our hands hold for a moment too long and his intense gaze makes me uneasy. Uneasy and utterly mesmerized.

When he finally releases my hand, I let out a shaky breath.

"Shall we sit?" he asks, nodding over to the sette.

I nod and follow him over to the small couch. Keeping my distance, I carefully sit down a couple of feet away and instantly clasp my hands in my lap.

"You're not what I expected," he murmurs, his voice low and almost to himself.

I can feel him studying me and I shift under his thoroughly penetrating gaze. "Oh? And what did you expect?" I ask, daring to look over and up.

He leans closer, eyes narrowing slightly. "Not you."

When he doesn't elaborate, I can't help but burst out laughing. Maybe it's my nerves making me be inappropriate or maybe I'm starting to feel a tiny bit more comfortable in his powerful presence. Which is the oddest thing. How can I be feeling less anxiety when I should be feeling more? But something about him is almost…I don't know. Familiar? We've never met, so I know that it makes no sense.

"What's so funny?" he asks, his eyes searching mine.

"I have to admit, I didn't expect this at all, either."

His mouth edges up and my attention zeroes in on that lone, beautiful dimple. "Really?"

I nod, unable to stop smiling. Maybe this situation isn't as bad as I originally thought it would be. Marrying a stranger still scares the bejesus out of me, but if he's a calm, kind, gorgeous man who can put me at ease and take his time, be patient with me, then perhaps I'd be willing to try.

"I know this whole situation is awkward," he says, as though reading my mind. "And our families are being…pushy. But, I want you to know, I'd never force a woman into marriage. If you're truly not interested in getting to know me better, I'll walk away."

"You would?" Of course, I lean forward and this makes me like him a little bit more.

"Before you make a final decision, you should know a few things first," he says, eyes bright and a little mischievous. "Some women consider me quite the catch."

"Oh, I'm sure," I say teasingly and chuckle. *Oh, my God, I'm flirting with him. And he's sitting here trying to sell himself.* A man this amazing and attractive certainly doesn't need to convince a woman to be with him, but here he is being all adorable and a little unsure. And, I like that. Confidence is nice, but arrogance is a huge turn off to me. I'm glad that he's wondering and maybe not quite as self-assured as he might normally be.

"That's right. They like the fact that I'm wealthy, powerful and, modesty aside, fairly attractive. That is, if you like the old cliche." The way he says it makes me grin. Almost like he's making fun of himself.

"Cliche?"

"Tall, dark and handsome." He sends me a devastating smile.

Oh, I do! I scream internally. More so than I ever even realized. But, I play it cool and send him a smirk. "Oh, I don't know. Normally, I prefer short, fair and homely." He knows I'm joking and his eyes crinkle in the corners in the most adorable way.

"Really?" He huffs out a laugh.

I shrug a shoulder. "But, perhaps, I could be persuaded to expand my horizons."

He slides closer and my heart threatens to burst from my chest when his powerful thigh brushes mine. I'm holding my breath as he reaches for my hand, lifts it to his lips and brushes a kiss along my knuckles. "Then I'll do my best to change your mind," he says in a low voice.

Swallowing hard, I bite down on my lower lip and a zap of awareness shoots through my body. The brief touch of his lips on my skin has me squeezing my thighs together and I can't seem to look away from his eyes. They're like a powerful, dark, swirling black hole, sucking me in deeper with every passing second.

The attraction between us is palpable and I smile. He's still holding my hand when he says, "So, Gia, tell me about yourself."

Gia? What is he talking about? *Oh, God.* My heart sinks as it belatedly occurs to my befuddled brain that I'm sitting here swooning over Miceli Rossi.

My sister's fiancé.

Oh, for God's sake. Then where the hell is the man I'm supposed to be marrying? And how am I ever expected to want him after meeting this amazing man?

"Um, I think there's been a mixup," I murmur, reaching for a piece of candy, and his dark eyes narrow.

2

MICELI

As I watch the most amazing creature I've ever met walk away from me, heading to meet a different man, I find myself fuming. Everything inside of me is rebelling at the thought of Alessia DeLuca going with Rocco Bianche.

First and foremost, I hate the prick. He's too cruel for someone as sweet as Alessia. He'll break her without thinking twice. Plus, he has a terrible reputation for treating women poorly. Bianche is abusive, both verbally and physically, and his previous girlfriend disappeared under mysterious circumstances.

Huffing out a breath, I stand up as the woman I'm supposed to marry walks into the room. Gia DeLuca is pretty and a couple of years older than Alessia. She gives off a calm, cool and collected vibe. Very elegant, well-dressed and chic. Perfect wife material, but I'm not interested. A muscle in my cheek twitches. I'm already missing Alessia and that artless air of innocence surrounding her.

"Gia?" I ask, making sure I confirm I have the right woman this time. The way this day is going there might be another sister that I'm unaware of.

"Sorry about that," she says, looking completely nonplussed. "I was told you'd be in the sitting room."

Her face is unreadable, a mask of indifference. And that tells me one very important thing—she really doesn't care who she marries. I'll do, Rocco will do...hell, any man from one of the Five Families will do even if he's old as dirt. Because it's clear she's already accepted her fate. Her job, decreed by Aldo DeLucca, her father, is to marry a powerful man from one of New York's most important mafia families and forge an alliance.

"I'm Miceli," I say and offer my hand. She takes it, barely, as though not wanting to touch me, and gives a very quick, weak handshake. And our future sex life flashes before my eyes. No passion, no love, no desire. She'll do her duty, of course, and give me heirs. But our time in the bedroom won't be leisurely and I'll need a mistress to take care of me. Because I enjoy fucking. And, if my wife doesn't then I'll have to go elsewhere.

Not a great way to start off a marriage.

My mind starts spinning. If Gia is indifferent to her circumstances then maybe Rocco and I could just swap fiancées. Unless Alessia is hitting it off with him right now. The thought makes my hand curl into a fist and I feel something I've never felt before—jealousy. I've never felt it over a woman, anyway. I've been envious of men with more power and money, sure. It's one of the things that's pushed me to work so hard. Because I want to be on top and, in order to do that, I need to crush my competition.

Which I do, gladly.

The ruling five mafia families in NYC, though technically my competition, are handled in a bit of a different way. Years ago, our grandfathers made a verbal agreement to stick to our own territories and businesses, and make a promise not to threaten or attempt to overtake anything belonging to The Rossi's, The Bianchi's, The DeLuca's, The Caparelli's and The Milano's. But within the last five years or so, lines have been crossed. Bodies have been found. And I think our shaky truce is about to go the way of the dinosaurs.

Which means I need to be ready to strike and to defend. If an all-out war happens then I will be the one to come out on top and rule this city. There is no other option. My main goal is to keep my family safe and out of harm's way. Along with that, I need to maintain a firm control on our assets and businesses, as well as our people. What I do on a daily basis…well, it's not a job for a man who has a weak stomach. My reputation precedes me and I've heard the rumors. People fear me and call me ruthless and cutthroat. I can't deny it. Because I'll do whatever has to be done. I've never been scared to get my hands dirty.

Or bloody.

It comes with the territory and I can accept it.

"So…" I motion to the couch where I was just sitting with Alessia. "Would you like to sit?"

With a polite nod, Gia glides over to the sofa and lowers herself, neatly crossing her slim legs. She's so controlled and beginning to remind me of a Stepford Wife. *Fuck.* That's the last thing I want. I need a woman who is passionate, vibrant and who challenges me. Not some cold statue-like creature who nods and agrees with everything that comes out of my mouth. I crave that fire and sassiness in a partner.

Stifling a sigh, I tell myself to give her a chance. But it's really fucking hard when I keep picturing her younger sister. Gia doesn't say anything, just waits for me to initiate the conversation. A conversation I don't want to have.

So, I decide to be blunt. "How do you feel about this situation?"

My question catches her off-guard. "What do you mean?" she asks carefully.

"You can speak openly, Gia. Because I plan to." I'm hoping that if I'm candid and matter-of-fact then she will be, too. Well, at least more so.

"Are you asking if I'm ready to get married?"

"I'm asking how you feel about marrying me? A complete stranger."

"My family expects it," she says simply. No ire, resistance or a trace of resentment fills her voice.

"And you're okay with that?"

"We all have to get married sometime, right?"

"Right," I say slowly, but it's not an answer to her question. It's me acknowledging the fact that Gia DeLucca and I would never have a happy marriage. The truth is, before today, I had no real interest in getting married at all, but I'm thirty-four and my parents are pressuring me. And even though they live at a winery over in Italy, it doesn't matter. They're up my ass constantly about finding a wife.

And I get it. But, at the same time, I want someone who makes me happy. Just marrying any woman isn't my goal. It would be nice to find a woman who I can talk to and maybe even love one day. I didn't come here expecting fireworks and love at first sight; I came here to fulfill my duty. The problem is Gia doesn't excite me and Alessia does. Alessia fascinates me in a way that no woman ever has before and now I'm wanting what I can't have.

Fuck that. I'm Miceli Rossi. I can have whatever I fucking want.

And, right now, I want Alessia DeLuca.

"Gia, this isn't going to work," I announce, standing up. She merely blinks, as though she knew this was coming. Or, maybe she's just completely indifferent. Who the hell knows? "Where is your father? I need to speak with him."

Gia stands up and smooths her hands down her perfectly-pleated pants. "I'll go get him." She pauses halfway to the door and looks over her shoulder at me. "For what it's worth, I agree. I think you're much better suited for my sister." Then she walks out, leaving me to ponder her words.

She thinks that? My heart thumps a little bit harder and I stand up straighter. *Interesting.* I'm not sure what I expected her to say, but I like that she's on my side.

After waiting a few minutes, both Aldo and Guilia DeLuca walk into the library. I have no idea what kind of relationship Alessia and Gia's parents have and if they actually love each other or were set up, too. My father mentioned something about Aldo being the only leader of the Five Families he could stomach, so that's why he's been pushing for me to meet Aldo's daughter.

"We heard there was a slight mix-up," Aldo says, but he's not smiling or making light of the situation. Which makes me wonder what Gia might've said. Gritting my teeth, I nod.

"That's right. I'd like to spend more time with Alessia," I say, cutting right to the chase. "I think we make a better match."

"Really? Even though she's ten years younger than you?"

"I don't see it as being a big deal, especially since Gia is eight years younger." My hackles raise and I get the feeling he's going to fight me on this. But, I'm prepared to win.

"Alessia has been promised to Rocco. His father and I spoke about this years ago and agreed. But you'll make a good match with Gia even if you don't think so right now."

My eyes narrow and my hands ball into fists. "I have to respectfully disagree, Mr. DeLucca. From the short amount of time I spent with your daughters, it's crystal clear to me that Alessia and I would be better suited. Nothing against Gia, but Alessia is who I want to make my wife."

There. Done. It's Alessia or no one. Let's see how the old man responds to that ultimatum.

DeLucca studies me for a long minute and I know he's trying to intimidate me, but that shit doesn't work. I'm younger, stronger and ready to fight for what I want. Even though it would be nice to have his respect, it's one of those things that won't be a deal breaker for me. With or without his permission, I'm going to move forward with Alessia. It would be super if we were all on the same page, but sometimes that doesn't happen.

"Are you saying it's Alessia or no one?" he asks, eyes narrowing.

"Yes, I am." There's no uncertainty in my statement, and I'm being completely forthright. Utterly transparent. He should respect my decision.

We lock eyes like bulls lock horns. I'm not backing down.

"Well, then I guess I will not be calling you my son in law. Have a nice life, Mr. Rossi."

What in the fuck? He just told me no? You have got to be shitting me? A determined fury spikes through my blood and before he can leave, I reach out and try again.

"Mr. DeLucca," I begin, striving to remain calm, "I'm sure as a married man, you understand the importance of connection and intimacy. Connecting with your wife and creating a strong and happy family together. I believe Alessia and I could have that together."

Aldo lets out a snort of disbelief. "You've known Alessia for five minutes. Tell me, Miceli, is it a happy family you crave or is it taking Alessia's innocence?"

Clenching my jaw, I realize the old bastard isn't going to give in. "I told you I'd like to get to know her better."

But he shrugs a shoulder. "You can get to know Gia better. Or no one."

21

My eyes dart over to Guilia, looking for support, but she merely gives me a sad look. It's clear she's not going to speak over her husband. *Fuck me.* Now what? Before I can think of what else to say, the DeLucca's walk out and I'm left standing there like a fool.

A fool who wants their youngest daughter badly. Badly enough that I'm willing to do just about anything to make it happen.

I guess I'm supposed to see myself out. With an annoyed sound, I straighten my suit jacket with a sharp snap and head to the door, pausing when I see Rocco Bianche shaking hands with Aldo and Guilia. And he looks so damn smug I want to punch him in his pockmarked face.

After a quick conversation, the DeLucca's walk away and Rocco spots me hovering in the doorway like a damn idiot. All I can think about is crushing him. Absolutely bringing him and Aldo DeLucca to their knees and destroying them in every possible way. And, I'd do it, too, if it weren't for that damn verbal agreement our grandparents made forever ago.

Hmmm. It might be time to forget about that. If I can't have Alessia, I can take this city. Conquer it. Make it all mine and fuck the other families.

The smirk on Rocco's ugly face has my blood boiling. Why is he acting like he beat me? There's no way he knows I want Alessia—unless he overheard my conversation with her parents. Barely suppressing a growl, I glare at him.

"Congratulations on your engagement to Gia," Rocco says, moving closer. "Had you met DeLucca's daughters before today?"

"No," I grit out.

"Yeah, me neither. I have to say, I'm glad we switched it up, though. I prefer Alessia's hot, little ass to her frosty sister."

It takes every ounce of control I possess to not punch him in the mouth. I don't say a word, but if looks could kill, Rocco Bianche would have already been shot, stabbed, gutted and fileted over a spit.

"I'm betting she's a virgin," he continues like the asshole he is, and I feel my control slip a notch. "Defiling pure pussy is my favorite pastime."

Keep it together, Rossi, I tell myself. "So, Alessia and you..." I search for the right word. "Clicked?"

"We will," he says without worry, waving a dismissive hand through the air. "She doesn't have much of a choice, anyway, does she?" His sharp bark of nasty laughter makes my skin crawl.

A devious thought slithers through my head: or, I could just kill you, motherfucker. And offer the poor girl a choice. Or, at least, an escape.

I give Rocco a tight, forced smile. Christ, I hate this asshole more than I ever thought possible. I'm going to have my private investigator do some digging on him. Already, I don't approve of him, but if I find out he killed his last girlfriend, which I suspect he did, you bet your ass I will be the first to share that news with Mr. DeLucca.

And I'll be the one who's laughing when Rocco Bianche goes straight to prison and I make Alessia all mine. Not that I don't plan to do that, anyway.

One way or another, Alessia will be mine.

3

ALESSIA

Well, that didn't go as planned. My heart thumps hard as I look out the window and watch Miceli Rossi walk down to his car. It's a big black SUV with dark-tinted windows, most likely bullet-proof, too. My family's home faces Central Park and I have a clear view from my bedroom window of the tall, dark-haired man who is going to marry my sister. He opens the door and slides into the backseat and then his driver maneuvers the car away from the curb and into traffic.

Ugh. My stomach hurts and my mind turns to Rocco Bianche. He is everything I don't want in a partner—arrogant, pushy, smug. I can sense a meanness just beneath his surface and I'm afraid he's the type of man who would snap for no good reason and take a perverse joy in punishing me.

I also don't find him the least bit attractive. He's average height with a soft middle and a hard face covered in acne scars. His thin lips seem to sneer a lot and I didn't appreciate the way his light brown eyes raked lasciviously down my body. He didn't even try to hide it and the way he was checking me out made my skin crawl. So skeevy.

I can't marry him and I told him so. After saying I couldn't marry a man I didn't love, the coldest look filled with hate flashed through his brown eyes. Then it disappeared and he gave me a tight smile. His parting words were simply, "That's a decision you'll regret. Think carefully and hard on it, sweet girl."

My skin crawls as I think back over our conversation, especially his parting words. But, I don't care what my parents want or push or demand. Rocco Bianche reminds me of a serpent, ready to strike, not a man I'd want to marry and raise a family with.

Now, Miceli Rossi, on the other hand, has my complete and undivided attention. There's no doubt in my mind that he's dangerous. Mysterious, too. But, something about him fascinates me. He oozes power and even a darkness, but it doesn't scare me. His energy draws me closer and I want to get to know him better.

Dammit. I can't believe I went into the library when I was supposed to go into the sitting room. How did Gia and I screw that up? Although, I was just doing what my mother said. So, technically, she's the one who messed up. I'm happy she did, though. It makes me realize what I want. And what I don't want.

And I know I don't want to marry a man who gives me bad vibes. I have no idea if the rumors about Rocco are true but if anyone would have the scoop, it's my best friend Cara. Turning away from the window, I grab my phone and drop down on my bed. Pulling her number up, I hit send and wait as it rings.

"Hey, A," she answers cheerfully. "What's up?"

Although Cara knows my family is pushing me to marry, I've never told her who they want me to be with. She doesn't understand the dynamics of the Five Families and the importance of maintaining and strengthening bonds with certain people. Her parents are lawyers, not mafia. But she does support and love me despite what my family does and I don't judge her either. Because, let's face it, my father has worked with her father to clear his name of certain things in the past.

"Cara, what do you know about Rocco Bianche?"

"Rocco? Isn't he the one who murdered his girlfriend?"

I curse under my breath. My friend is an all-star gossip and has the most brilliant ways of finding out information and deciphering fact from fiction. "I don't know. Are the rumors true? Because he's the man my parents want me to marry."

"Nooo! Are you serious?"

"As a heart attack," I answer glumly.

"Oh, holy shit, Less. You can't marry that guy. He's a monster."

I sigh and start picking at my comforter. "I was hoping you could tell me something different. Have you heard anything good?"

"About Rocco? God, no."

"There has to be something. It's not like he eats children for breakfast and murders puppies."

"No, just girlfriends."

"I was hoping that wasn't true."

My friend's voice lowers to a conspiratorial whisper as she says, "All I know is he had a girlfriend named Mercedes who mysteriously vanished after they had a big fight. Nothing was ever proven one way or another and no criminal charges were ever brought against him because there was no evidence. None found, anyway. Like I said, she just…disappeared."

A shiver runs through me. "Do you think he killed her?"

"You want the truth?"

"Of course."

"Personally, if he didn't do it himself, I think he hired someone to do it. Most likely one of his men."

"This isn't making me feel better."

"I'm sorry."

"The thing is my parents want a marriage between me and a son of the Five Families. So, they chose Rocco for me...and Miceli Rossi for Gia. There was a mixup, though, and I met Miceli first."

Cara waits patiently for me to continue, but I'm not sure how to explain the fact that Miceli intrigues me like no one else ever has before.

"Aaand," she prods, stretching the word out in anticipation.

"And I've never met anyone quite like him," I admit. "Everything about him is..."

Utterly delicious.

"Is what?"

I huff out a breath. "I don't know how to explain it. I'm just really curious about him."

"Uh-oh. It sounds like you want Gia's fiancé."

"I mean, technically they aren't engaged yet." I'm trying to find ways to justify my feelings and Cara isn't stupid.

"What makes Miceli so much more interesting than Rocco?" When I don't answer right away, she laughs. "You think he's hot, don't you?"

"Yes. He's ridiculously beautiful in every way. What do you know about him?"

"Just that he's just as dangerous as Rocco. Probably more so."

I sigh, not wanting to hear that.

"Have you talked to Gia? Maybe she'd be willing to do a swap." When Gia chuckles, I frown.

"It's not funny. This isn't a joke. My parents are really expecting an engagement and marriage. This is my life we're talking about, not just some random date."

Cara quickly sobers up. "I'm sorry. I guess I'm just having a hard time wrapping my head around the fact you're supposed to marry a man you don't know. The whole idea of your parents promising you to someone you've never met is pretty damn archaic."

"I know, but they're counting on strengthening alliances within the Five Families. And somehow that's fallen on my shoulders. And Gia's."

"Can't you just tell them no?"

A sharp laugh rips from my throat. "Yeah, right. They'd probably disown me. Or, give me the biggest guilt trip of my life."

"But, it's your life, Alessia. Not theirs."

"I know," I whisper, mulling over her words. My future happiness is at stake. And if I marry Rocco, something deep down tells me it's going to be a bitter, nasty and very unhappy union. And, I might wind up disappearing just like Mercedes.

"If you're giving in to your parents' demands, at least choose a man who interests you. Please, Less, don't go with Rocco. He's not a good person. There's always a kernel of truth to rumors."

"What should I do?" I ask, feeling trapped and unsure.

"Talk to Gia first. See how it went with Miceli. Maybe she has no interest?"

"Okay. Thanks, Cara." My sister does seem to be rather indifferent about the entire situation.

"Anytime! And keep me posted!"

After promising to let her know what happens, I drag myself off my bed and head down to Gia's bedroom. Poking my head in, I knock lightly on the doorframe. My sister is curled up in a chair, scrolling through her phone. "How'd it go with Miceli?" I ask curiously, walking inside.

Gia looks up. "He's very handsome."

Jealousy stabs through me and I try not to react. "Did you have a lot in common? Was he nice?"

Gia tilts her dark head, studying me closely. "He wasn't very friendly. And he kept asking questions about you."

That grabs my attention. My ears perk up and I think my heart stops beating in my chest before speeding up like crazy. "Me?"

"What the heck did you do in five minutes that made him totally infatuated? Because he wasn't interested in me whatsoever."

My mouth drops open and I hurry forward, sitting on the edge of her bed, eagerly leaning forward. "Are you serious? You think he likes me?"

"No doubt about it. He'd rather be with you and he made that abundantly clear."

A part of me is shocked to hear this but, at the same time, it's like I already knew it.

"Was he rude or did he hurt your feelings?" I ask, brow furrowing.

"No, he just let me know where his interest lies."

Secretly, I can't help but be pleased. "There seemed to be a connection between us," I admit slowly. "More so than with Rocco."

My sister's eyes narrow. "Don't fool yourself, Lessi. They're both dangerous men who have a history of doing very bad things. They steal, lie and kill. All for the sake of power."

Deep down, I know she's right, but I don't want to let myself think those things about Miceli. However, it's easy for me to believe such atrocities about Rocco.

"I know," I say in a low voice. "I honestly don't think I'm ready to get married, anyway. Especially not to a complete and total stranger. I'm not exactly the most experienced person in the world."

"You've never had a serious boyfriend. It only makes sense that you'd want to fall in love and be intimate with a man you have strong feelings for first. Before being sold off like a cow to the slaughterhouse."

"I suppose that's one way to put it," I comment dryly.

"Once you have sex it isn't that big of a deal anymore," she tells me wisely. "But when you're still a wide-eyed virgin with hopes and dreams about finding your soulmate, you want your perfect match. But, trust me. All men are the same."

Ever since my sister and her boyfriend Marcus broke up, she's lost the glow she used to have. Now, she's jaded and dull. It makes me sad that things didn't work out because she's turned into someone who no longer believes in love and happy endings.

"I don't believe that," I insist. "If that's true then it shouldn't matter who you end up with."

Gia gives me a sad look. "It doesn't."

Wow. My sister is even more dead inside than I realized. "I want to choose who I give myself to and, preferably, to a man I'm in love with. Why can't Mom and Dad understand that?"

"Because they had an arranged marriage, too."

Even though I already know this, I never dwell on it. I suppose it explains a lot, though. They seem to get along and are companionable, but I'd hardly say they're head over heels in love with each other. Half the time, my father sleeps in the guest bedroom at night, claiming his back hurts, and I don't remember them ever saying I love you.

And I know that is not the kind of loveless relationship I want to have with my future husband.

So what exactly am I supposed to do? Ask Gia if she'd like to swap fiancés? That hardly seems fair or right, especially since Rocco isn't a good guy. Running a hand through my long hair, I let out a frustrated breath.

"I don't want to wind up like them," I say softly. "If I can't choose my own husband then I'm not getting married at all. Especially not to a man who has a reputation worse than the devil's."

Gia cocks a thin, dark brow. "And how exactly do you plan on getting out of this?"

"I don't know," I answer honestly.

"I only see one solution."

"What?"

"Leave," she says simply. "Go far away from here and take control of your life."

As scary as that idea is, there's something very appealing about it, too. I'd have to leave New York City, find somewhere safe to go, get a job so I could pay for an apartment, food, clothes, a car. All my life, I've depended on my father to pay for everything. But with freedom comes a price, right? I'd have to break the chains holding me to the DeLucca fortune.

The thought terrifies me. Yet, at the same time, it's also so exhilarating.

Chewing my lower lip, I wonder if I can do it. Could I really leave my family and all this behind?

"Why haven't you left?" I ask Gia. "You don't seem happy." And, it's true. All the spark and grit my sister used to possess is gone. It's like her light has gone out and she's just a husk of who and what she used to be.

For a long moment, she doesn't say anything. Then she gives me the saddest, smallest wisp of a smile I've ever seen. "After losing Marcus, I just don't care anymore. About anything. Father could marry me off to Satan himself and I'd accept." Her dark eyes glisten with unshed tears. "I'm broken, Lessi. Please, do whatever you have to do, but don't end up like me. Like a woman who doesn't care if she lives or dies."

Getting up, I pull my sister into a hug, angry at myself for not realizing how deeply hurt and lost she's become after losing Marcus. "I won't," I promise.

Gia is right. The only way to avoid becoming a sad, unhappy woman like Gia is to run away. To take my life and my future, into my own hands.

It's suddenly very clear to me that I need to escape from here as soon as possible.

4

MICELI

s the day passes and evening approaches, my obsession with making Alessia DeLucca mine grows from a small fire to a raging inferno. I've always enjoyed a good challenge and never backed down or shied away from anything that was difficult. So, that's how I'm viewing this situation—as the ultimate challenge.

Do I deserve her? Maybe yes, maybe no. That's not the point. Hell, I am no angel and I've certainly done my share of bad things. But I had to in order to stay in control and on top. The moment you show weakness in this world I live in, an enemy will come out of the woodwork to stab you in the back then slit your throat. It's brutal and ruthless and, in order to survive and thrive, you need to be willing to do whatever it takes.

This isn't about whether I'm deserving, though. What it boils down to is I need a wife eventually, and I want Alessia now. I'm drawn to her innocence and feel a potent chemistry. And what I want, I always get. However, her parents aren't exactly cooperating. The fact that Aldo immediately shut me down really sticks in my craw. He should accommodate my wishes, not annoy me. Plus, I have that pain in the ass Rocco Bianche to deal with. *Prick.*

Drumming my fingers on the large, dark wood desk in my corner office at the winery's headquarters, I sigh. I'm used to getting my way. Sometimes it takes a little persuasion or even greasing some wheels, on occasion. But, I don't have the time or patience for that right now. Rocco is sniffing around my woman, trying to steal her away from me.

And that isn't acceptable.

Jerking up out of my leather chair, I stalk over to the enormous window, cross my arms and look out over the Manhattan skyline. I run so much in this city, but it doesn't belong solely to me. And that irks me. Out of the Five Families, the Rossi's deserve it all. Supreme control. We help maintain the peace, work incredibly hard and keep everyone else in line. And it's not an easy job.

But, if I had the total respect and control I should, that I've fucking earned, then Aldo DeLucca would be jumping up and down with joy and gratitude, welcoming me as his new son-in-law. But, no. The old bastard is challenging me. Denying me.

Dropping my arms, I clench my fists. Aldo is going to learn the hard way that I don't take no for an answer. I'm going to come up with a plan to make Alessia mine, get her away from that asshole Rocco, and marry her.

I figure I have two options. One, I could eliminate Rocco so they can't get married or two, I could seduce Alessia and make her mine. Taking her innocence and possibly knocking her up would seal the deal real fast. Aldo would be begging me to take her off his hands then. Debating between the two, I think the more logical solution would be to seduce Alessia. I'd rather not have Rocco's blood on my hands because it would break the truce and most likely cause an all-out war between the Five Families. Besides, I felt Alessia's attraction and the intense chemistry between us. Luring her into my bed shouldn't be that difficult. And it'll be a helluva lot more enjoyable than hunting Rocco down and killing him.

Mind set, a plan begins to form. But, I have no patience. With thoughts of Alessia's long, dark hair and stunning blue-green eyes in my head, I decide to leave work early—something I rarely, if ever do. If I leave the office before seven, it's a miracle. And even then I'll get home and keep working on my laptop or have a meeting that I need to attend.

A billionaire mafia man's work is never done. And it's important I keep my eyes on everyone surrounding me at all times because no one can be trusted. They'd usurp my throne in an instant. Today, however, at six o'clock, I stand up, grab my briefcase full of endless papers and reports and sling it over my shoulder. Instead of calling down to my driver to pull out in front and wait for me, I give him the rest of the night off. My personal SUV waits down in the garage below and I plan to drive myself tonight. Because, well, what I'm about to do is highly embarrassing and I don't need any witnesses.

The elevator takes me straight down to the subterranean garage and I walk over to my Range Rover, pressing the key fob to unlock the doors. I like to keep several different cars so no one will know which one I'm in or what one I'll use. Sometimes it seems a little silly, but better to be safe than sorry. I'm not a man who likes to show his cards. A little mystery will keep 'em guessing. It will also keep me safe.

The engine roars to life, I pull on my seat belt and put the car in drive. With evening traffic, I anticipate it will take me a while to get from the Financial District all the way up to Central Park where the DeLucca's live. Which is perfect because then the sun will have set and I can sneak around under the cover of darkness.

Sneak around. I shake my head. I'm not sure what the hell is going on up in my brain, but I'm desperate for a glimpse of Alessia. It's like this weird obsession has come over me and I need to see her. Since I can't exactly walk up to the door and talk to her like a normal person, I'm resorting to the next best thing—stalking.

Technically, I wouldn't classify myself as a stalker quite yet. It's still too early for that messy label. But the desire to see her is overwhelming. So much so that I'm about to sit in an hour or so of traffic that is crawling along at a maddening pace. I'm not sure how my driver stands this shit. But I take comfort in the fact that I pay him exceedingly well.

By the time I reach the DeLucca's brownstone, my stomach is growling because I didn't have time to eat lunch earlier. I pass by the home and it's lit up like a Christmas tree. Pulling aside, I wait, parked illegally, to see if someone is going to vacate a parking spot any time soon so I can snag it. Parking in this city is a bitch, but I find that people are coming and going all the time. If I'm patient, a spot eventually opens and then I'll snap it up quickly.

Exactly three minutes later, a sedan pulls away from the curb almost directly across from the DeLucca's house. I hit my gas pedal and zip over. In one smooth move, I parallel park the large car, turn it off and focus my attention on the house. The curtains are all open on the first floor and I lean forward, my nose practically pressed to my tinted window, as I search for a glimpse of Alessia.

Pathetic? Maybe. But ask me if I give a shit.

The longer I watch the neighborhood comings and goings surrounding the brownstone, I definitely begin feeling like a first-class stalker. And, the longer I sit here and the more people that pass by make me wonder if I've lost my everloving mind. I have never done anything like this before but, even after telling myself to leave, I don't move. I fucking can't. Because I still haven't seen my sweet girl yet.

After what feels like forever, movement on the first floor catches my eye. From my position, it's hard to see exact details and I'm beginning to wonder if I should get some binoculars.

Oh, hell. No, I tell myself, *you aren't doing that.*

There's something kind of exciting about waiting for a glimpse of Alessia. Like an addict about to get his next fix. However, like all highs, this one eventually wears off. Over an hour and a half later, I haven't seen her—not even a glimpse—and I'm starting to get annoyed. What did I expect, though? A clear view straight into her bedroom? Getting lucky enough to see her stand in front of the window and look out? A glimpse of her undressing? Seeing that soft, creamy, naked skin of hers?

My dicks thickens, pressing against my zipper. With a groan, I adjust myself and my stomach growls again. A quick glance at my watch and I see it's getting late. I need food and it's probably best if I just go home. I'm not exactly good at this stalker thing and I'm not even sure what else I can do.

You could kidnap her, a little voice whispers.

The tempting thought fills my head and I'm actually considering it when I see a car pull up at the end of the block. There's a rideshare light glowing through the back window, but I don't think too much of it. Deciding it's time to leave before I do something incredibly stupid, I turn my car on, fasten my seatbelt and see a small figure sprint up and emerge from between the DeLucca's house and their neighbor's place.

Squinting through the darkness, I notice that the figure is slight and I immediately conclude it's a woman. Her head is covered in a hood and it's pulled low to hide her features. But the moment she steps beneath the street lamp, the light lands on her and I can just make out Alessia's delicate bone structure.

Attention glued to her every move, I watch as she jogs down to the corner and slips into the Uber. She's also carrying a small duffel bag and my heart lodges in my throat. Where is she going? I wonder.

Deciding to follow the Uber, I pull away from the curb and keep my distance, but still remain close enough so I don't lose them. All sorts of questions plague me and I'm beyond curious. Where is she running off to?

Then a very disturbing thought hits me. What if she's going to visit a lover or her boyfriend? My gut clenches with anger and jealousy. Maybe she isn't as innocent as I'd originally thought. Biting down hard, I follow them and realize we're heading back downtown again. The blocks zip by and traffic is much lighter now because it's getting late. After what feels like forever, the Uber pulls up in front of the entrance to Penn Station.

Huh. Of course, there's nowhere for me to park, so I do the only thing I can. Act like a crazy man, throw my car in park, turn my hazard lights on and jump out. "Alessia!" I yell and she spins around, eyes wide in shock.

Hurrying around my SUV, I step onto the sidewalk, heading straight toward her.

"Miceli?" She blinks in surprise. "What're you doing here?"

That's a damn good question. I can't exactly tell her I was sitting outside of her house and then followed her here.

"I need to talk to you," I say, deciding to keep it vague.

"Okaaay," she says, drawing the word out, her sea-blue eyes large and so damn pretty.

"Where are you going?" I arch a brow, studying her closely, and instantly see the guilt wash over her slightly flushed face.

"That's not really your business," she states, turning cool.

I disagree, but don't bother saying so. Instead, I step closer. "Will you come with me? So we can talk?"

"We don't have anything to talk about," she insists, and for the first time it occurs to me that this situation—that Alessia—might be more difficult to manipulate than I'd originally anticipated.

"You're wrong. Because Rocco Bianche isn't the right man for you. You can't marry him. I won't let it happen." I don't care if I come off as arrogant or bossy. She needs to come with me and listen to what I have to say. I glance over at my car, double-parked in the busy street. Preferably, she comes with me before I get a ticket from a passing cop.

"You're right. I'm not marrying Rocco."

My stomach jumps at her revelation. "No, you're not. You're going to marry—"

The word "me" gets cut off when I notice a quick movement from the corner of my eye. But it's not normal movement like a passerby. My gut tells me it's a threat and I react accordingly.

The car with blacked out windows slows to a stop and a man jumps out. His lower face is covered in a bandana and he locks eyes on us. When he begins to approach, I spot the gun in his hand right away and dread washes over me. Spinning, moving on instinct, I lean down and reach for the pistol tucked in the ankle holster I always wear. At the same time, the man picks up his pace, lifting his weapon.

Fuck. Without thinking, I dive forward, crashing into Alessia and we roll across the pavement. Yanking her behind a vendor cart that sells pretzels, I shove her down behind me, using my much-larger body to cover her. "Stay down!" I hiss, lifting my weapon.

Shooting a gun on a busy sidewalk full of pedestrians isn't something I'm eager to do, so I wait. Apparently, I'm the only one who thinks this is a bad idea because the asshole stalking towards us fires off one... two...three shots.

Panic sets in and people scream and run for cover. Luckily, the shots only hit the cart. Still though, it's too damn close for comfort and I need to get Alessia out of here. Needing to stop this asshole, I fire off two quick, carefully-aimed shots. One hits him in the leg and the other slams into his chest, bringing him down.

Without a word, I stand up and close the distance between us with a few, long-legged strides. He'd gotten far too close and we barely averted disaster. All I can think about is this bastard just tried to cut me down, but I'm used to this kind of shit. It comes along with the territory. Alessia, on the other hand, didn't ask for any of this and the idea of her getting hurt, caught in the middle of a gunfight, fills me with a red-hot rage.

Stopping beside the groaning man, I kick his side hard enough to crack ribs. Then I raise my gun and put another well-placed bullet in him. This time, in the center of his forehead.

When an enemy comes after people I care about, I don't hesitate to eliminate them. And with zero fucking mercy.

5

ALESSIA

My hammering heart and the pop of bullets echoes so loudly that I squeeze my eyes shut and plug my ears. On my hands and knees, hidden behind the vendor cart, I'm in shock and my entire body shakes. I didn't expect the man to start shooting in the middle of the sidewalk at Miceli, and that tells me he has very dangerous enemies.

Even though my father runs in the same mafia circles, no one has ever tried to execute him on a public street full of witnesses. I've never experienced anything like this before and it's terrifying.

Miceli returns fire—I didn't even know he had a gun—and the man drops. At this point, I'm thinking we should jump into his car and leave. Instead, Miceli walks straight over, viciously kicks him and fires two more times. And I'm ready to curl up into a ball and start crying.

I'd like to think I'm made of tougher stuff than this, but when bullets start flying and suddenly your life flashes before your eyes, my bravery all but vanished. Fear like I've never known before washes over me. Then Miceli walks back over and pulls me up off the ground. He wraps a strong arm around me as he guides me quickly over to his car. I'm still feeling a little dazed, so I'm grateful for his arm around my waist because I might fall over without its firm support.

"Get in," he orders, opening the passenger door.

Moving on autopilot, I slip into the SUV. After quickly securing my seatbelt, I realize I'm breathing hard and shaking like a leaf. Miceli gets in on the driver's side, the locks click and he spins the wheel, maneuvering us away from the scene of the crime.

Squeezing my hands tightly, I send Miceli a sidelong glance. His profile is stern, mouth set in a grim line, and he's focused on the street ahead. It occurs to me that the man I wanted to get to know better— that I was considering getting engaged to—just murdered a man with zero hesitation or remorse.

Slowly, my senses start coming back to me. Then, they come flying back all at once, hitting me like a splash of ice-cold water. *I'm sitting next to a cold-blooded killer.* I reach for the door handle and yank up.

"Let me out," I order, hoping my voice sounds firm and not weak.

"No." His voice is flat, emotionless and unwavering.

I spin and glare at him. "What do you mean no?"

"No," he repeats in a clipped tone.

Not sure how to respond, I cross my arms and glare at him. How dare he? Not only has he messed up my plans to run away, now he's taking me further away from the train station. "I need to go back and—"

"You're staying with me."

His tone brooks no argument, but I'm not giving up so easily. This is ridiculous. Pulling in a deep breath, I say, "I appreciate you getting me out of there, but this is all your fault." One of his thick, dark brows shoots straight up.

"Oh?" He practically growls the word, but I'm not scared of him. Although, I probably should be. But, deep down, I know Miceli wouldn't harm a woman. I believe that with every fiber of my being. He's not Rocco Bianche.

"I had a plan, a train to catch."

"And where do you think you were going?"

"That's none of your business. But, far away from here."

"You weren't sneaking out to visit a lover?" he demands.

"What? No." I frown in confusion. "What're you even talking about?" *A lover?* Is he crazy? I've never even been kissed. But, of course, I don't tell him that.

"I saw your bag," he says, nodding to the duffel bag I somehow managed to grab and not leave behind in the chaos.

"Because…" My voice trails off. I don't want to relinquish my secrets.

"Because you were running away?" he presses, slanting me a steely look.

"No. Maybe. It's really not your concern." Wow, he flusters me like no one else.

"Alessia," he begins as though speaking to a small child. "Why did you sneak out after dark and take an Uber to Penn Station?"

Instead of answering, I grumble a stubborn, "Let me out," between clenched teeth.

"You're a stubborn little thing, aren't you?" His mouth edges up and, if I didn't know better, I'd say he's amused.

"Me? I just want out. You're the one refusing to listen."

"Oh, I'm listening, little girl. I'm just not changing my mind." Before I can comment, he continues, "In case you missed it, there was a bad guy with a gun. And, I promise you, where there's one bad guy, there's more."

A shiver races down my spine. I really hadn't thought about it that way, but I refuse to tell him that.

"So, you're welcome, princess."

My jaw drops. Okay, so maybe he did "sort of" rescue me, but I don't appreciate the derogatory nicknames. Besides, he's the whole reason people were shooting guns in the first place. So, technically, this is all his fault. "I'm not a princess. Or, a little girl."

He turns and his hot gaze slides down my body. "No, you're definitely not a little girl." His voice turns husky and the heated look in his dark eyes makes me swallow hard. "But you are a mafia princess. Whether you like it or not."

"I don't want anything to do with that world," I tell him, crossing my arms over my chest..

"It doesn't matter what you want. You were born into it. Trust me, when your family is mafia, there's no escaping it."

"Well, I would've escaped it if you hadn't just ruined my plans." I'm still miffed about missing my train. But, at the same time, I sit back and eye my rescuer closely. God, he's so good-looking. But in a dark and very dangerous kind of way. He's a man who clearly straddles the line of morality, and if this were a book or movie, I'd have no idea if Micelli Rossi is the hero or the villain.

"If I hadn't stepped in, you'd be dead." His voice is matter of fact.

"They weren't after me," I say and roll my eyes.

"How do you know that?"

His words take me by surprise. I had assumed the hitman wanted to eliminate Miceli. But what if he's right? Me? *Oh, God.* Why would anyone want to kill me? What did I ever do? No. Miceli had to have been the intended target. That's what I believe, but I don't say anything more. Instead, I turn in my seat and focus on his rugged profile.

"You do realize the police are going to arrest you now."

"No, they won't," he states without a trace of worry.

"You just killed a man."

"Only because he tried to kill me first. And you. That's called self-defense."

I let out a huff. "I know what it's called, but they're going to at least want to question you."

"I have friends in high places," he tells me arrogantly. "I'm not worried which means you shouldn't be, either.

"I'm hardly worried." Actually, the only thing that currently concerns me is returning to the family brownstone. I start chewing my lower lip and worry fills me. Without realizing it, my knee begins bouncing with nerves and Miceli glances down at the telltale movement. When I see him looking, I instantly stop and swallow hard.

"What's wrong?"

"Are you taking me back home?" I ask, dread filling me. "So you can tell my father?"

Miceli turns and arches that black brow of his again. "Is that what you want me to do?"

I shake my head. "No. I want you to take me back to Penn Station so I can—"

"Not happening."

I let out another frustrated huff. "So, if you're not taking me back to the train station and you're not taking me home then where are we going?" When he doesn't immediately respond, I scrunch up my nose and point out the window. "How about that bus stop over there?"

"I have somewhere much safer."

Leaning forward, I tilt my head. "Where?"

"My house."

I blink in surprise, not quite sure that I heard him correctly. "Wait, what?"

He makes an annoyed sound, fingers tightening around the steering wheel. "I didn't plan for things to go this way, okay? But the situation has changed, so we're going to adapt."

"I don't understand," I murmur, sending him a bewildered look. "What do you mean?"

"You're not marrying Rocco Bianche!" he practically yells, slamming on the brakes and stopping for a red light.

I jerk forward, the seatbelt pulling tight against my body, and brace a hand against the dashboard. That is the last thing I expect to hear him say and, maybe I'm mistaken, but Miceli almost sounds... jealous.

"Well, no," I say slowly. "Why do you think I was leaving? The last thing I want is a loveless marriage to a man I don't know."

A muscle flexes in his jaw and I notice him visibly tense. But he remains quiet, not commenting further. After a long moment, he sighs and looks over at me. "Sometimes we have to do things that we don't want to do. It's called a sacrifice."

"I know what it's called," I snap. "But why should I be expected to give myself to a complete stranger?"

"To strengthen your family's alliance with my family."

Again, I think I misunderstand him for a brief moment. Until what he's saying begins to slowly sink in. But, no, he must've spoken wrong. "Your family?" I echo. "But I was supposed to marry Rocco."

"You're not marrying Rocco," he grits out.

As I mull over his words, a dull throbbing starts at the base of my skull. Miceli is going to get engaged to Gia, so I'm not sure what this has to do with me. Suddenly, I'm so confused. My head hurts and I massage my temples.

At the next light, I hear Miceli blow out a breath, then his hand reaches over and wraps around my thigh. I jump, not expecting his touch, and his long fingers lower, hovering near my knee.

"What happened?" he demands, voice low and angry.

Leaning forward, I glance down and see my leggings are torn. My knee is scraped up and bleeding. "Oh, I didn't realize," I say quickly. "I'm so sorry. I don't think I got any blood on your car."

Miceli frowns. "Fuck my car. We need to make sure your knee is okay."

His concern catches me off guard. But, in a refreshingly nice way. I can't remember the last time someone showed worry for me like this. "Oh, um, it'll be okay. I honestly didn't even notice it until you said something."

"As soon as we get to my place, I want to clean it up. You tore your knee up on a dirty Manhattan street, princess. There's no telling what kind of germs could get in there and infect it."

Wow. It occurs to me that Mr. Rossi is concerned about my well-being. And here I thought he would yell at me for getting a blood stain on his expensive leather seat. I sneak a glance over at him and give him a little smile. I think it's really sweet that he seems so concerned.

His black gaze locks on mine and I realize his fingers are still wrapped around my leg. He gives my leg a squeeze then returns his hands to the steering wheel and his attention to the road. Meanwhile, my heart is beating out of my chest. Something about Miceli Rossi warms my blood in the most delightful way.

"Where do you live?" I ask quietly.

"Just up ahead," he states. His voice is so low, it rumbles, and I can feel it way down deep, vibrating through my body. And I love that.

Leaning forward, I glance through the windshield and see we're coming up to Billionaire's Row. It's a collection of the swankiest, most expensive realty in Manhattan and only a select few can afford to live here. "Which one?" I ask, looking up at the impressive highrises.

Miceli points to the tallest, most modern looking building of the group along West 57th Street.

"Holy crap," I murmur, and he chuckles.

"A tower fit for a princess," he murmurs, and I glance over at him.

"Why didn't you take me back home?" I ask, my pulse rate speeding up. That seems like the most logical thing to do, yet here we are at his fancy-shmancy apartment building.

"Several reasons," he says mysteriously.

"Care to elaborate?"

He shrugs a shoulder. "First and foremost, you're not marrying Rocco. Second, my place is very safe. And, third, I decided it's best if you're with me."

With him? What does that even mean by that?

"Oh, you decided? For how long?" I ask.

"Until I say, princess." Miceli tosses me a wicked smirk. "Consider yourself kidnapped."

6

MICELI

ven though I keep my tone light, I'm not kidding. I'm
kidnapping Alessia and not letting her go. Not ever again,
but she doesn't need to know that quite yet. All sorts of
plans are swirling around in my head and I have to take my time and
do this carefully. I don't want to frighten her, but the fact of the
matter is she's not marrying Rocco which I already told her—she's
marrying me.

And there's not a damn thing anyone can do to change my mind.

Once I pull my car into the subterranean garage and the gate lowers
behind us, I feel much better. My building is like a fortress and no one
is getting in here. I can protect Alessia and keep her safe without
worry. The building boasts 24-hour armed security, endless cameras
and requires keys and codes to get practically anywhere. Including the
elevator which will zoom us straight up to my penthouse. I grab her
duffel bag and we walk over to the elevator and step inside.

After placing my key in its special slot and turning it, I hit the 129th
floor then lean back, resting a hand on the railing, my attention
moving over to Alessia. Her chest rises and falls fast and her amazing

blue-green eyes are wide. She looks nervous, like a little rabbit who is on the verge of bolting.

"You're safe now," I tell her, trying to make her feel more secure. "I promise, no one will harm you here."

She gives a small nod and wraps her arms around herself. Damn, she looks so small and dainty. So delicate. More fragile than the soft petals of a flower. Anyone who tries to lay a finger on her will have to deal with me. With my wrath. And I will not show them an ounce of mercy. In fact, I'll enjoy breaking every single one of their fingers... right before I cut their whole damn hand off.

I've always had a protective streak toward my family, but Alessia is bringing out an even stronger, more ferocious side that I didn't know existed. For now, she'll be safe here with me. This building is like Fort Knox and no one is getting in who I don't want inside. Then, once we move forward together and get married, my name will protect her. Because no one in their right mind fucks with a Rossi. If they're stupid enough to do so, they will pay the consequences. And that's a fucking guarantee.

Alessia doesn't say a word the entire way up and I hope she's not going to fight me about staying here and letting me protect her. And, of course, there is the little part about her becoming my wife. But, hell, if she was even considering marrying Rocco, then she should have no problem marrying me. I'm a much sweeter deal. I will treat her like a princess—give her anything she wants including expensive gifts like jewelry. I'll keep her wrapped in furs and whisk her away on exotic locations anywhere in the world where she'd like to go. Basically, I'll spoil her rotten. Oh, and I'll give her endless orgasms, make her lose count as I pleasure her every day and every night.

Her air of innocence is one of the things that draws me to her. It's wrapped around her like the sweetest perfume, teasing me and making me want her more than I've ever wanted anyone else before.

My gaze drifts down her body, over each perfect curve, and I want to rip her clothes off and mark her. Make her mine.

Patience, Miceli. Hell, I feel like a stallion on the verge of rutting. The temptation to spin her around, lift her up and slam deep inside her from behind has me sweating and getting hard. Clenching my hands, I force myself to relax and my attention drops to her knee where her leggings are torn and bloody.

All thoughts of fucking her shut down and white-hot anger infuses me. Who would dare attack us on the street in front of everyone? I'm livid about the entire situation and plan on calling a meeting with the Five Families to address the issue. For all their sakes, what just happened better have been a random fucking incident or there's going to be hell to pay. I will release fire and brimstone like they've never seen before.

The elevator stops and the door glides open, letting us out in my private foyer. I motion for Alessia to exit first and try not to look down at her ass. Too late. It's so fucking round, pert and impossible to ignore, and I ball my hands into tight fists, forcing my gaze back up. *Juicier than a peach.*

The dim lighting automatically brightens as the sensors read our presence. Even though Alessia has always been surrounded by wealth and comfort her entire life, her eyes grow round as saucers. I drop her bag and enjoy the way she looks around with curious eyes and obvious admiration.

"Wow," she murmurs under her breath.

My place is pretty amazing, but I guess I take it for granted. It's the tallest residential building in the world at 1550 feet, a perfect combination of power and delicacy, boasting top-notch amenities and security. I have the best views available—from river-to-river—and there's nothing I can't see, depending on which window I'm looking out of. From the Financial District to Central Park to the nighttime sky above, I have a kick-ass view of the entire city.

I watch Alessia walk further inside, taking everything in, and she heads straight to the enormous floor-to-ceiling windows.

"This is incredible," she says in a low voice, admiring the nighttime view of the entire city. Moving up beside her, I want to tell her to get used to it because she's going to be living here from now on, but I don't dare. It's too early for that conversation.

"I'd think you'd be used to places like this." Although, deep down, I know her family isn't nearly as wealthy as mine. It's probably another reason why Aldo wants to marry his daughters off to me and Bianche. Our wealth far surpasses his own and he wants to make sure they're taken care of. Though, I wouldn't trust Rocco Bianche any further than I could throw him.

"Are you kidding me?" she asks, glancing up at me. The light above hits her eyes just right, making them glitter like aquamarines floating on the ocean surface. I suck in a breath, unable to look away.

"Your eyes are so beautiful," I whisper.

Alessia blushes and quickly turns her attention back out the window. "Thank you." She tugs her full lower lip into her mouth and chews on it.

"Do I make you nervous?" I ask in a low voice, stepping closer. The last thing I want is for her not to be comfortable or pull away or distrust me.

She shifts from one foot to the other then turns to face me. Damn, she's so little, barely coming up to my shoulder. "A little," she admits.

"What can I do to make you more comfortable?" I ask earnestly, searching her unsure gaze.

"I don't know. I mean, you're a stranger and I'm still not sure what I'm doing up here in your fancy apartment."

"You're here because I want you here. And because I'm protecting you," I quickly add. "Now come with me. I need to clean your knee up."

"It's really not that bad—"

"Let's go." I reach for her hand and pull her along with me through the living room and down a wide-open hallway. One of the things I love about this place is the open floor plan and cathedral ceilings. I hate feeling closed-up and walled-in; I much prefer feeling the freedom of fewer walls and large windows.

She doesn't bother trying to argue with me and it's for the best because she won't win. Not when it comes to making sure she's well-cared for and comfortable. I'm not sure what has come over me, but it's become my goal to make sure this small woman is happy, content and safe in every way possible.

Tugging her into a large, first-floor bathroom, I nod toward the marble counter. "Hop up there." She briefly hesitates then does what I say as I bend over and fish out a First Aid kit from beneath the sink. Popping the latches, I take a quick inventory of the items and pull out what I need.

Turning toward Alessia, scissors in hand, I have a feeling she isn't going to like this next part, but it's necessary. "Don't move," I say and reach for the torn material of her leggings. She sucks in a breath, but holds very still as I cut up the side seam on one side, effectively turning them into biker shorts. Half of them, anyway.

I peel the shredded, blood-stained legging off, toss it in the trash and kneel down between her legs, focusing on her bloody, scraped up knee. It isn't awful, but it needs to be cleaned thoroughly. Grabbing some alcohol and cotton balls, I douse them.

"This is going to sting," I warn her, and she gives a brave nod. Then I carefully start wiping. She lets out a small hiss and I feel awful, but I don't stop. Once I'm done, I blow lightly on the wound. "You're okay, sweet girl. So brave."

Without thinking, I run my hand over her calf and press a kiss to the side of her knee. Alessia goes completely still and I look up at her through hooded eyes. Our gazes lock. Setting her small foot on top of my muscled thigh, I blow on her knee again, soothing the sting away. "Better?" I ask huskily. Something flares in her ocean-colored eyes and she nods.

"Thank you," she murmurs softly, voice a little unsteady.

I give her calf a light squeeze then reach for a Band Aid. Keeping her knee propped up on my leg, I tear it open and very carefully cover her wound, pressing the adhesive edges into place against her skin. Skin so soft that I can't help but steal a caress. Then I reach for the scissors again, moving her other foot up onto my thigh, and start cutting up the seam of her leggings.

"We should even them out," I tell her with a slight smirk. I can't say I've ever cut a woman's clothes off before, but I'm enjoying it thoroughly. From the heated look rising in her blue-green eyes to the way I'm holding her leg, her foot sliding up, and now so damn close to my groin. *Shit.* My dick is starting to get involved and pushes against my zipper, desperate for her.

Time to put an end to this, I reluctantly think, as I peel the other legging off and toss it. Jaw clenched, dick throbbing, I force myself back up onto my feet and turn before she can see the evidence of my desire. Although, I have a feeling it may be too late. A gorgeous shade of pink brightens her cheeks and she swallows hard.

I offer my hand and help her slide off the counter. "C'mon. It's getting late and you've had a traumatic evening. Let's get you settled." *In my bed,* I carefully and purposely leave unspoken. But, that's exactly where she'd headed.

Her small hand feels so right in mine and it briefly catches me off guard. This wisp of a woman is making me feel all sorts of things that I've never experienced before. It's odd, yet strangely soothing, and I find myself welcoming it.

Guiding her up the back staircase, I lead her down to the master suite. I hope she finds it just as impressive as the rest of the house. Though it's not nearly as spectacular as she is, it's pretty grand with a huge king-sized bed positioned to face the windows, sleek black furniture and decor all in black and white with hints of gray. I opted not to have any pops of color because I'm not what I consider a colorful person. I prefer strong, solid, classic colors. It occurs to me that I prefer most everything in my life like that—from my decor to my suits to the aftershave I wear. I don't care for frills or fads. Give me opulent elegance with staying power.

"Is this the, ah, guestroom?" she asks hesitantly, looking around.

"No. This is my room." I'm not going to lie or play games with her and the sooner she accepts her fate, that she belongs to me, the better off we'll be.

"Um…" Her gaze lands on the bed draped in a black comforter. "You must have a spare room for me?"

Of course, I do. But that's not the issue.

"I'm not letting you out of my sight, Alessia," I tell her, voice firm. "Rest assured, my building is safe, but I won't be comfortable if you're not near me."

"That's nice," she finally says, "but not necessary."

And here it comes…my princess is about to fight me. "It's necessary for me and my own piece of mind."

"Miceli, I am not sleeping in the same bed as you."

"Yes, you are."

"No—"

I move fast and grasp her upper arms, my long fingers easily curling all the way around her small biceps. "Princess, you are going to get your ass in that bed and go to sleep. And that's non-negotiable." My voice softens. "I promise I won't touch you...if you don't want me to," I can't help but add.

Her brow draws together and I can feel her nerves grow.

"I promise," I whisper again, this time more fervently, and she seems to relax slightly. *For tonight, anyway,* I mentally add. "Now, let me go get your bag. Meanwhile, go ahead and use the bathroom. There are clean towels and a new toothbrush in the medicine cabinet. If you need anything else, let me know. Okay?"

She nods. "Okay."

I can hear the hesitation in her voice and I understand her fears. But I'm going to put those fears to bed and make sure no one hurts her. Ever. Because the more I think about it, the more I believe that hitman wasn't coming after me.

I think Alessia was his intended target.

7

ALESSIA

I'm still in the bathroom, stalling, when I hear Miceli moving around in the other room. Needing my duffel bag, I open the door and step into the bedroom. My attention instantly moves to Miceli who has removed his suit jacket, tie and is currently unbuttoning his black dress shirt. He looks ridiculously good in all black and I swallow hard as he slips the dress shirt off and turns, sensing my presence.

Holy Mary, Mother of God. My gaze dips, soaking up his firm, muscled chest and then drops to his insanely flat, ridged abs. No one should have such a perfect and enticing body. He looks like a freaking sculpture carved from marble. His hands reach for his belt, those long fingers slowly loosening it, and I watch, absolutely mesmerized. It takes quite a bit of effort to pry my eyes from that dark strip of hair disappearing down into his pants and when I realize where I'm staring, my cheeks burn hotly and I glance back up to see his lips twitching.

Oh, my God, he thinks this is funny. I probably have the most dumbfounded, slightly idiotic look on my face, so I can hardly blame him for wanting to laugh. I've never seen such an amazing display of potent masculinity in person and my hands itch to run over each groove and muscle.

Clearing my throat, I grab my bag and disappear back inside the bathroom fast. Before he removes those perfectly-pressed slacks and really gives me something impressive to look at. *Gah.* Shaking my head, I dig my pajamas out and hurriedly change. Meanwhile, I start popping my watermelon hard candy because I'm so damn nervous, I can't see straight.

Glancing into the huge, spotless mirror, I realize my shirt is a little too thin and my bottoms are a little too short. It's not exactly skimpy, but there's something a little teasing about my sleepwear. Until now, I've never thought too much about it because I've never had anyone to tease.

A nervous flutter fills my stomach when I open the door and step back into the room. I know the instant Miceli's gaze lands on me because my entire body begins to heat up. I've never been so aware of another human being in my entire life. Daring to glance over, I see him standing near the bed, wearing a pair a black, long silky pajama bottoms and, of course, he's shirtless. Something I could get used to really fast.

I can feel his eyes moving up and down my body, and it's impossible to ignore. A part of me even enjoys the attention. Setting my bag in the corner, I finally turn to face him and he's moving across the room, closing in on me like some kind of stealthy, very hungry panther.

"Let me take that," he says, reaching for my bag. "In the morning, we'll hang your clothes up in the closet with mine."

Taken aback, I watch him deposit my bag in the huge walk-in closet with his clothes. Why would we be hanging up my clothes? I don't plan on staying here long enough for that. "That's really not necessary," I start to say.

"I want you to be comfortable," he insists.

"Miceli, I don't think you understand. I'm leaving tomorrow and—"

"No," he interrupts, "you're not."

"You can't just kidnap me!" I huff out a breath and cross my arms which in turn lift my breasts higher. His black eyes immediately dip, filling with heat, and I glance down to see my pebbled nipples on display. *Dammit.* I immediately uncross my arms and make a frustrated sound.

Meanwhile, Miceli stalks closer, until he's standing directly in front of me, and he places a finger beneath my chin, tilting it up. Forcing me to look up into his midnight eyes.

"Call it whatever you want," he murmurs, gaze locking with mine. "But here's the situation—I don't think that man was trying to kill me. I think he was after you."

I gasp and shake my head. "Why would anyone be after me?"

"You're a mafia princess and belong to one of the most powerful families in the city. There are a million reasons."

I'm stunned and suddenly my legs feel a little wobbly. Reaching up, I slide a hand around Miceli's thick wrist, holding onto it for support or I'm scared I might fall down. His words leave me unsteady and full of questions..

"I won't let anything happen to you," he promises, his voice low and making my body react in strange ways. Releasing my chin, he takes both my hands in his, holding them firmly, and the gesture makes me feel instantly secure. "You're cold...and shaking. C'mere, princess."

The moment he pulls me into his arms, wrapping me up in the heat of his huge body, I melt against him. Maybe I should push him away and demand that he release me, but I like knowing I'm safe here. Especially if someone is after me.

Burying my face against his hard, warm chest, I wrap my arms around his back and hold on for dear life. Suddenly, I'm scared. What if someone is trying to kill me? How am I going to live my life without constantly looking around every corner and being scared all the time? I suppose I could have a bodyguard, but that's a last resort. I like my privacy and can't imagine being followed around all day.

After what feels like forever, but is probably only a couple of minutes, Miceli pulls back. His dark eyes drop to my mouth and my heart slams against my chest as his head begins to lower. *Oh, my God, he's going to kiss me.* I can see his intention clear as day. And I want it. I want his lips on mine so badly that I'm burning up for it. The moment his lips touch mine, it's like a flare goes off inside my body. Everything lights up and becomes alive in the most amazing, inexplicable way. Sighing softly, my lips part slightly and he deepens the kiss, tongue sliding inside and meeting mine.

And it's electric.

I've never kissed anyone before and it becomes clear very quickly that Miceli is a master kisser. I do my best to match his moves, touching my tongue against his, and to learn from him. My body, wearing only thin pajamas, is pressed against his, practically wrapped around him, and, as we're kissing, I feel his hard cock push against my belly. Oh, wow. He's rather large and—

Miceli tears his mouth away and curses under his breath. I'm not sure why he swore, but he releases me, takes a step back and eyes me warily. And it occurs to me that I might've messed up somehow.

"Did I, ah, mess up? I'm sorry. I don't have much experience kissing men." I frown, my attention dropping to the light smattering of dark hair on his chest. God, he's sexy. Maybe I should be completely honest. "Actually, no experience. You're sort of my first."

He utters another curse and swipes a hand through his dark hair. But, it occurs to me that he doesn't look upset. "That was your first kiss?" he asks, dark eyes glowing. He steps closer. "Me?"

Disbelief fills his voice. I am twenty-four years old and the epitome of a late-bloomer in nearly every way. Especially when it comes to men. A sudden shyness overwhelms me and I manage a nod. Miceli reaches out and cups my face with large, gentle hands.

"I can do much better than that," he murmurs. "Let me try again?"

Better? Is he kidding? "Okay," I whisper, beyond curious. "but that was pretty good."

He smirks then leans in and captures my mouth again. Taking full control, he angles my head back, tasting and nibbling for a moment, then sweeping his tongue past my lips and drinking deeply.

Oh...my...God...

The way he kisses me has me moaning and writhing in his arms. His kisses are steamy and all sex. Wetness pools between my thighs and everything around me turns hazy and dream-like as he continues to explore and plunder. It almost feels like he's marking me. Claiming me on some primal level.

When Miceli finally releases my mouth, I tighten my grip on him or I might fall over. He pulls me back up straight and his mouth edges up. "Better, right?"

Try out of this world, I want to say, but I don't want to stroke his ego. Instead, I smooth my hands down my rumpled pajamas. "Not bad," I say, trying to pull myself together and not swoon.

"Not bad?" he echoes, his dark, thick brows pulling together in a scowl. Before I can tell him I'm teasing, he hauls me up, spins me around and pushes my back against the wall. Not expecting the sudden move, I wrap my legs around his waist and hang on. His large arms cage me in, palms flat on either side of my head, and his mouth slams against mine. The restraint he showed earlier is gone and this is a completely different kind of kiss. It's rough, dark and exciting. And, so very demanding. I slide my fingers through his hair, tangling them in the thick, black strands, and feel his hard erection press against my core. He rotates his hips, grinding against me and I gasp into his mouth.

It all feels so new and so good. Pushing my breasts against his bare chest, I squirm against him. Needing and wanting so much more. Then, with a growl, he yanks his mouth away and stares at me, breathing hard.

"Better?" he grits out, his hips bumping against mine, making me completely aware of his very large cock thrusting against my core. Hell, there's no way I can miss it. Just like his mouth, I have a feeling his cock is quite demanding.

"I was just teasing before," I admit, trying to catch my breath. "All of your kisses were amazing. Mind-blowing, actually."

"Vixen," he hisses then slowly lowers me to the floor. His eyes slide closed and he looks like he's in pain. "Get in bed. I'll be right with you."

"Where are you going?" I ask.

"To take care of my weeping cock."

My mouth drops open at his blatant honesty and I watch as he limps toward the bathroom and closes the door. A certain amount of satisfaction washes through me as I walk over to the bed. I did that to him. I made the big, powerful mafia man weep.

Pulling the covers back, I crawl into bed and I hear a muffled groan from the bathroom. Goosebumps break out over my skin and I yank the sheet up to my chin. *You can bring this man to his knees, Alessia.* I'm not sure where the thought comes from or if it's even true. But, it's interesting to consider—a woman's sexual power over a man. Until tonight, I've never experienced just how incredible it can be. I can see how it could almost be…addicting.

When the door opens again, my gaze slides down Miceli's perfect chest and drops to the front of his silky, black pants. He took care of the issue and I find myself wondering how long it would take to get him all worked up again. What if I reach out and touch him? Stroke him through those satiny pants?

I have no idea where these wicked thoughts are coming from, but one thing is certain. Miceli Rossi is causing a sexual awakening in me that I can't seem to control. Nor do I want to.

True to his promise, Miceli doesn't touch me at all during the night. And, the funny thing is, I'm disappointed. I find myself craving his kisses, his warm touch, the way he made me feel so lost in a haze of desire.

There's no doubt about it—I don't like how far away he's sleeping from me and I wonder why he's keeping his distance. But, I find myself enjoying the soft, steady sound of his breathing and the way it lulls me to sleep. And I love how when I snuggle down into his sheets, his scent surrounds me. It smells expensive, extremely masculine and I can't deny the way it makes my stomach flutter. Being here with Miceli, I've never felt so protected, so safe. In fact, this may be the best night of sleep I've had in a very long time.

When morning comes, my eyes flutter open and I realize I'm alone. Reaching over, my hand falls on the spot where Miceli slept. It's still warm and I miss his presence. Considering I didn't want to stay here in the first place, it's an odd thought to have.

Just when I'm wondering what to do, the door opens and Miceli walks inside. He's wearing a black silk robe and carrying a tray with coffee, tea, orange juice and several pastries. My stomach instantly growls. I didn't eat dinner the other night because I was too nervous before running away to the train station, so now my belly is reminding me how hungry it is.

"Good morning," he says, walking over and setting the tray on the bed then crawling in beside me. "I wasn't sure what you like, so I brought you a few choices."

His kindness touches me on a deep level and I smile shyly. "Thank you. This is very nice of you." And it is. The gesture makes my chest tighten with emotion. No one has ever treated me like such a...well, a princess. Miceli is so attentive to my every need and it's definitely something a girl could get used to very fast.

"You're welcome." He lifts a mug filled with steaming hot coffee and takes a drink, watching me thoughtfully over the rim.

I reach for the glass of orange juice and take a small sip, watching him right back beneath my lashes.

Miceli lets out a soft sigh. "We need to talk."

"About what?" I ask, wishing he'd just shut up and kiss me again.

"About today..." His dark eyes search mine, "and the fact that we're getting married."

My jaw drops. "What?" I burst out, not quite sure that I heard him right. My fingers tighten around the glass then start shaking so hard that I have to set it back on the tray. "What're you talking about?"

"No one will dare try to hurt you if you're mine. My name will protect you."

I shake my head back and forth. "That's not a reason to get married! And what about Gia? She's the one you're supposed to marry."

"I'm not marrying Gia," he states darkly. "I'm marrying you. If you go back home now, your life will be in danger. They will hunt you down, find you and kill you to hurt your father. Is that what you want?"

"No, of course not!"

"Good, then it's settled."

As he takes another drink of coffee, looking slightly smug, I cross my arms. "Nothing is settled. I am not marrying you or Rocco or anyone else. Only a man that I choose."

"Well, you better choose me fast, princess, because the priest is scheduled to arrive in…" He glances down at the large watch on his wrist, "exactly twenty minutes."

"What?" I jump out of bed. "You are crazy!" Turning, I race for the bathroom, ready to lock myself up in there and refuse to come out when a strong pair of arms wrap around my waist and haul me back against a very muscular chest.

Miceli's lips lightly touch the shell of my ear as he whispers, "Be a good girl, Alessia. Don't forget, as my wife, your job is to honor and obey."

"I am not your wife!" I slam a foot down, stepping on his insole, but he doesn't even flinch. I'm so mad I could spit. "Let me go!" I order.

Instead of releasing me, his hand curves up over my breast, cupping it possessively. "You're mine, Alessia, and the sooner you realize that, the better off you'll be."

Then, without warning, he spins me around in his arms and slams his mouth down against mine in a kiss that knocks the wind from my lungs. I struggle for about three seconds before melting against his hard body. Damn him.

And damn me.

Because, clearly, I have no restraint when it comes to Miceli Rossi and his spellbinding kisses. Kissing him back hard, I twine my fingers through his hair and yank hard enough to make him growl. Then I bite his lip, though not enough to actually hurt, and he pulls back with a chuckle.

"You're even more feisty than I thought." His eyes seem to darken even further, though I'm not sure how that's possible. They already resemble a moonless night. "We're going to get along just fine. In every way."

My traitorous body heats up at his huskily-murmured words.

"Now be a good girl and get dressed. You have fifteen minutes and if you don't come down, I'll come right back up here to get you. And, believe me, when I say a locked door won't keep me away from you, Alessia." His voice drops. "Nothing will."

A shiver runs through me and I know he's right. About everything. From the moment we met, something unexplainable happened. And now it seems that our futures have been intertwined. Determined by something much stronger than us. *By Fate?* I wonder.

The truth is I find myself not really minding all that much. But I would never admit that to Miceli. No. If he forces me to marry him, I'm going down that aisle kicking and screaming. And if he is arrogant enough to think this is going to be easy, he's dead wrong. With a half smile, I slowly walk away, my hips swaying a little extra, and I step into the bathroom, closing the door behind me. Then I lock it.

Bring it on, Miceli, I think and pop a hard candy into my mouth. If you want me, come get me.

8

MICELI

The moment I hear the lock engage, I grind my teeth. She's going to make this difficult. I already know it and I reel in my anger. There's no use getting upset about it, though. It's not really a surprise that my princess can turn into a headstrong pain in the ass. But, honestly, I wouldn't have it any other way. I enjoy her fire and her fight. It bodes well for our sex life, too. I've never been attracted to meek women. I like a challenge and I certainly like a woman to give as good as she gets in the bedroom.

I understand why she doesn't want to marry me—or anyone—at this moment. Hell, I'm a total stranger, but that will be changing fast. I plan to get to know everything about Alessia. And I mean everything. From her favorite foods to the way she sounds when she comes and everything in between.

I've never taken the time to truly get to know a woman before and figured I'd save that for whoever I make my wife. Now that I'm on the precipice of marrying Alessia, a part of me can't believe it's actually happening. I haven't told anyone except my butler Piero who is currently downstairs whipping up a celebratory meal. My family is going to flip their shit when they find out, but I'm going to keep this my secret for a little while longer. Or, at least, for as long as possible.

After quickly dressing in my usual black shirt, suit and shoes, I smooth my thick, slightly wavy hair back with a bit of gel and splash my face with some aftershave. My breath is minty fresh and I lean closer to the mirror in the guest bathroom, examining my teeth to make sure nothing is caught between them. God, I'm nervous. And, that's odd for me because I'm never nervous about anything. Confidence reigns supreme in my everyday life. Anxiety and nerves belong to the weak.

"Mr. Rossi?"

I turn around and walk into the attached guest bedroom to see my butler. Although calling Piero a butler is quite an understatement. He is a jack of all trades and takes care of everything for me—from the cooking to my schedule to making sure everyone else does their job. Quite honestly, I'd be lost without him. And right now he's carrying several small velvet boxes.

"What did you find?" I ask, reaching for the first one. They're potential rings for Alessia and I need to choose one fast. Since time is of the essence, I had Piero call the local jeweler, describe what I wanted and rush the rings over for me to look at and choose.

"Several very nice options," Piero says. He starts opening the other boxes and setting them up on the dresser. "I suggest you make a quick decision because Father Francesco just arrived and is waiting patiently in the living room."

"Let him wait," I grumble, snapping the first box shut, not at all happy with the diamond. It's far too small. Grabbing the next one, I frown. "I said a big diamond."

"They're four carats. That is considered rather big," Piero tells me, and I frown.

"Not big enough for Alessia." So far, all of these rings are boring, far too small and plain. None of them will do. Then I pick up the last box and pause, my attention finally snagged. It's a large, brilliant diamond with a ruby on either side. The combination is fiery and stunning. Just like my Alessia. "This one."

I snap the lid shut and tuck the ring in my inside jacket pocket.

Piero nods knowingly. "I had a feeling that might be the one."

"Tell Fr. Francesco we'll be down momentarily." I pull in a steadying breath and start heading back to my bedroom. "I have to break my reluctant woman out of the bathroom first."

I hear Piero try to stifle an amused half snort-half laugh and fail miserably. Rolling my eyes, I stalk down the hall, enter the master suite and pause, hands on my hips, debating the best way to handle the situation. *I did warn her,* I think, and decide to try doing this the easy way first.

"Alessia?" I pause in front of the door, placing my hands on the door-frame. "Are you going to open this door or make me break it down?"

No answer.

Narrowing my eyes, I grind my jaw. We're one-hundred and thirty floors high, so there's no way she climbed out the window and made a break for it. No, my stubborn princess is simply ignoring me like the brat she can be.

"Alright, fine," I grit out. "You want to do this the hard way then—"

The door opens and Alessia stands there, looking up at me. "There's no need to break the door down," she states, looking unhappy.

I hate that she looks...well, if I'm being honest, slightly miserable. Maybe the ring will perk her up. Women like sparkly shit, right?

"Alessia," I begin evenly, "I know this is far from normal, but every-thing will work out. You have to trust me." Before she can respond, I drop down on my knee, reach for her hand and lift it up, holding it against my chest. "Even though we don't know each other well yet, your father wanted our families aligned more closely through a wedding. I met you first and felt a connection right away. I hope you felt something, too?"

Alessia looks a little in shock, but forces a small nod.

"Good. We can build off that and I promise to be an attentive husband who treats you with respect and kindness. Trust me, princess, I will never hurt you. I'll take care of you, protect you and worship you."

She swallows hard as I reach into my jacket pocket and pull the velvet box out. Flipping the lid open, I make sure she gets a good look at the ring. Her gorgeous, sea-swept eyes widen. So far, so good. Plucking the ring out, I slide it onto her finger. It's a little big and we'll have to get it sized correctly.

"I want you to be my wife, Alessia."

"What about what I want?" she whispers and I narrow my eyes, feeling everything in me go tight with anger.

"You don't want me?" I snap, my restraint coming undone.

"I want a choice," she insists.

"Too bad," I say without thinking my words through. "You don't get a choice. You get me as your husband and that should be more than enough."

Alessia pulls her hand away and sends me a scowl. "You can't force me to—"

"Watch me!" I stand up, grab her around the waist and toss her over my shoulder. Alessia cries out and slaps her small fists against my back.

"What're you doing?" she demands, trying to twist away.

"Making you my wife. Now behave!" I slap a palm against her ass and she gasps, immediately going still.

Then she turns into a demon, kicking and twisting. "If you force me to marry you, I will be the worst wife you've ever had!" she threatens.

"I've never had a wife," I reply dryly. And, hell, now I can see why I was never in a rush to deal with this bullshit.

Marching out of the bedroom and down the hallway, I pause at the top of the stairs. Okay, so maybe I'm being a bit of a domineering ass, but I'm pissed. What the hell is the problem? I see how women watch and swoon over me. How they attempt to seduce me into their beds. Any woman in her right mind would marry me in a damn heartbeat and this feisty, little shit is acting like it's the worst thing in the world.

"Are you going to walk down these stairs?" I ask, loosening my grip. Giving her a chance. "Or, am I going to have to carry you down?"

"You are the biggest jerk I have ever met!" she declares angrily and hits my back with a balled-up fist. "Now put me down before I scream!"

I let out a frustrated growl and start marching down the stairs, and she bounces against me. "Oh, trust me, you'll be doing a lot of screaming," I hiss, "later on in my bed."

That settles her down and I carry her into the living room where Fr. Francesco sits, waiting patiently. His eyes widen when he sees us and I pretend there's nothing unusual about having a woman slung over my shoulder.

"Father Francesco, it's nice to see you. I'd like for you to meet my fiancée, Alessia."

"Oh, uh…" He stutters and stands up, circling around me and leaning over until he's eye to eye with the little brat hanging down my back. "It's a pleasure to meet you, Alessia."

"Hello," she murmurs politely.

Well, I'm glad she's at least being nice to the old man. Rolling my eyes, I shift her body and turn to face Fr. Francesco. "Can we get this started? Before my bride decides to try to run off?" I crack her ass again and she lets out a squeal.

"Put me down!" she orders.

"Of course," Fr. Francesco says, reaching for his prayer book. "But, Miceli, you may want to do as the young lady says and please put her down. I'd like to believe this is consensual so I can give you both the Church's blessing."

"It's consensual," I tell him. "She's just having a temper tantrum."

"I never said yes," she reminds me tartly. For whatever reason, her words sting and I flinch. "And, may I also remind you that you didn't actually ask."

Huh. Well, I suppose she does have a point there. Thinking back, it occurs to me that I more demanded than requested. *Shit.* I suppose I better fix this quickly. I glance over at Fr. Francesco. "Can you give us a moment?" I ask. He gives me a nod and walks out, pulling the door shut behind him. And, I swear, I hear the wily, old bastard mumble a "good luck" under his breath.

I slowly lower Alessia to the floor and look into her sea-colored eyes where a hurricane currently whips around. "You're right," I immediately concede. "I've never proposed to anyone before and I did a pretty bad job, didn't I?"

"It wasn't great," she admits quietly, twisting the too-large ring around her finger. "You didn't even ask."

"I got down on one knee," I remind her, "and declared my hopes for our future. I gave you a big, expensive diamond."

"And then declared you wanted me for your wife. I like having a say in my life, Miceli. It's the whole reason I ran away in the first place.

Because my parents weren't letting me decide my own future. You need to understand how important that is to me."

"I understand…and I'm sorry. Sometimes, I can be a little bossy."

"A *lot* bossy," she corrects me.

"That, too," I admit, mouth edging up. "When I want something, I go after it hard. Full-force. And, I'm not going to lie and play games. I want you, Alessia." I let out a breath, lower myself back onto one knee and reach for her hand again. *Take two.* "Alessia, will you marry me?"

I wait with baited breath for her answer. If she says no, I'll probably just force her, anyway. But, it won't be pleasant for either of us. Or, Fr. Francesco, for that matter. I shift, looking up at her, waiting patiently. And, she sure takes her damn time. Just when I think she's going to tell me to go to hell, she slowly nods her head.

"Yes, I will marry you, Miceli."

Relief pours through me because I was ready to do battle. Without thinking, I squeeze her hand, bring it up to my lips and brush a soft kiss against her knuckles, whispering thank you.

Now that everyone is in agreement—or Alessia, anyway—I call in Fr. Francesco and Piero who will serve as our witness. The ceremony goes surprisingly smoothly and fast. In less than ten minutes, we listened to a short scripture passage, declared our undying love and exchanged vows.

"Congratulations, Mr. and Mrs. Rossi," Fr. Francesco declares, grinning from ear to ear. "You may kiss your bride."

I turn toward Alessia, slide my hand around her neck, cupping it gently, and kiss her. Not wanting to put on a show, I keep it restrained and fairly quick. But, I enjoy the sweet, fruity taste of her hard candy. It's over before it begins and we say goodbye to Fr. Francesco. Piero has us sign the marriage certificate and then it's done. At least the official part, anyway. Now, we can move onto the good stuff. The part where I take Alessia into my bed and fuck my new wife until she's screaming my name.

"The celebratory brunch is all ready," Piero tells us, grinning widely.

Oh, right. I suppose it is still only eleven in the morning. Too early to drag Alessia back to bed, especially since we just got up not long ago. Still though, I wouldn't mind calling it a day sooner rather than later.

"Are you hungry?" I ask her.

"Yes."

Her voice comes out soft, almost shy, and I take her hand and lead her down to the large, modern kitchen. Sun shines in through the skylights and I tell Piero to serve us in here rather than in the formal dining room.

We sit down at the small kitchen table with a metallic silver top, and I stare at my bride, a little amazed that I actually went through with the ceremony. And that I was so vehement and domineering about the whole thing. I'm not exactly sure what came over me, but Alessia makes me a little crazy and a lot possessive.

And now she's mine.

Glancing down, I notice her twisting her ring. "We'll get that sized for you," I tell her and she nods.

Suddenly, I'm not sure what to say. The truth is I behaved like a brute and practically forced her into this, completely strong-armed her into this marriage. Will she resent me for it? I want our lives together to be pleasant. But did I take things too far? Does my wife hate me already?

The thought makes my gut twist. I plan to make up for my outlandish behavior and hopefully multiple orgasms will soothe her. Otherwise, I'm not sure what to do. Maybe start buying her more jewelry. That always seems to work with women.

Although, I have a feeling my fiery, little wife isn't like most other women. And, I'm not sure how well that bodes for me.

9

ALESSIA

Piero serves us a delicious breakfast of blueberry pancakes, sausage, bacon, hashbrowns and fresh fruit parfaits. And, of course, I eat way more than I should. But from the heated looks my new husband keeps sending my way, I have a feeling that I'm going to need all of my energy and then some later tonight.

My new husband. The words reverberate through my head and make me a little dizzy. I can't believe I'm married. Even harder to believe is that I'm married to Miceli Rossi. Just yesterday I had my first kiss and now I'm his wife. In what world does that happen? It's definitely going to take some adjusting and I can only imagine what my parents are going to say. God, they're going to flip out. Which brings me back to the fact that no one else knows about this yet.

Unable to eat another bite, I slide my plate away. "That was delicious."

"Piero is an excellent cook," Miceli says, eyeing me closely. He still looks hungry, but not for food. For me. A small shiver runs through my body.

"How is your family going to handle this? Us, I mean?"

Miceli shrugs a broad shoulder. "Does it matter? It's over and done with and, ultimately, it's not their decision. It's mine."

"Hmm," I murmur.

"What?" he asks, leaning closer, his elbows resting on the edge of the table. "What's that mean?"

"Well, you did take all of the decision-making into your own hands." His handsome face screws up into an annoyed scowl.

"Are you going to keep reminding me of that?"

"Probably." I reach for a blueberry and pop it into my mouth. "But you brought it on yourself."

"You're going to be very happy as Mrs. Miceli Rossi," he informs me arrogantly.

I arch a brow. "Oh, really? And what makes you so sure?"

"Trust me, princess. After tonight, you won't be going anywhere. And you'll have no doubts that you're exactly where you belong."

I'm not sure how he can be so confident, but it may be up to me to knock him down a few pegs. "If you say so," I murmur without much conviction, and his dark eyes immediately narrow. "I want to know more about your family."

"Like what?" he asks warily.

"Tell me about your parents and siblings. You're the oldest, right?"

Miceli settles back in his chair and nods. "I'm turning thirty-five this year and I do my best to keep everyone else in line. But, they can be an unruly bunch."

"I'm sure…if they're anything like you," I add teasingly. "Does your family live in the city?"

"Not my parents. Salvatore and Carmela live on the winery back in Sicily. They're very old school."

"How so?"

"They prefer speaking Italian and are more comfortable living a more simple life, surrounded by their roots and friends. They avoid the city and never come to New York. I run all the businesses here in the States."

I nod, interested in learning more about Miceli's family. "And brothers and sisters?"

"I have three younger brothers and a baby sister. Vincentius is thirty-two and he's the most sensitive one of us. Enzo is thirty and he's the sophisticated one. Angelo is twenty-eight and a player. Every time I talk to him, he has a new girlfriend. And, Carlotta is twenty-five and the baby of the family."

"She's a year older than me," I muse, hoping we can meet and become good friends. A strange look passes over Miceli's face and I get the feeling he just realized his wife is younger than his baby sister. *Awkward.*

Miceli clears his throat. "And, like I said, my parents stay in Sicily. We go over there when we want to visit. And we always celebrate the holidays together over there. Christmas in Sicily is beautiful."

"Are you close to your family?"

"Extremely. What about you and Gia? Are you close?"

"We used to be," I answer honestly, feeling a pang of guilt. I still wish I had paid more attention to her after her terrible breakup with Marcus. But, I just assumed she'd get over it. I mean, he wasn't that great and I really never understood what she saw in him. "But, lately, she's pulled away."

"Why?"

"There was a guy she was dating and he broke her heart. She hasn't been the same since. I didn't realize how bad it was until…"

"Until?" he presses.

"Until she didn't care whether she married you or Rocco. She's become so sad and distant. It breaks my heart, but I'm not sure how I can help her."

"Time and hindsight should help. Also, finding someone new and better can't hurt."

"Well, if you know anyone," I joke. "Maybe we can all go on a double date."

Miceli chuckles. "I'll let you know."

A companionable silence falls over us and then Miceli's cell phone rings.

"Excuse me," he murmurs and answers the call.

From what I can hear, it's a business call and while he talks, I take a moment to surreptitiously admire my new husband. As much as he has the power to annoy me, Miceli also has the power to make me come undone. Without a doubt, he is the most attractive man I've ever seen. His long fingers curl around the phone and his expression is serious as he speaks in a firm tone. He oozes intelligence, control and an authoritative presence. No wonder people defer to him in this city. He's competent and radiates a palpable power.

Unable to look away, I study his thick, dark brows, nearly black eyes, straight nose and sensuous mouth. He's clean shaven, but I can already see dark stubble growing in and it's sexy as hell. I remember the dark smattering of hair on his chest and the powerful build of his body. Knowing we're going to be together tonight in the most inti-mate way possible sends a bolt of lightning straight through my center and right into my core. I can't deny how much I enjoyed his kisses and the way his hands felt on my body. A shiver runs through me and his gaze meets mine.

And they're burning with barely-suppressed desire.

Good God. Liquid heat fills me and I swallow hard. The truth is, I want my husband, but at the same time, I am a little scared. I can admit I've been a bit of a headstrong brat these past twenty-four hours, so I am a little unsure about how he might retaliate. Is he going to be rough and make me pay for fighting him so much? Or, will he be gentle? Even though I haven't told him I'm a virgin, he's probably guessed the truth. How could he not? Until yesterday, I hadn't even kissed a man. So, I think it's a pretty safe assumption that I've never had sex with one either.

After another minute, he disconnects the call, still eyeing me closely. The heat and tension seem to be building around us and I shift in my seat.

"So, ah, what did you want to do this afternoon?"

"Do you really have to ask?" His voice is deep and husky.

I blink in surprise. "You can't be serious?"

Miceli abruptly stands up. "Serious as a heart attack."

"But…" I'm not sure what to say. "It's barely noon," I finally stutter.

"I don't care what time it is." He extends his large hand. "I'm taking my wife back to bed."

My stomach flip-flops and I'm not sure if I'm ready for this now. "But we've barely talked." I'm grasping for excuses and his eyes narrow.

"We can talk later." He grabs my hand and tugs me up onto my feet. "Don't make me carry you."

Hurrying to keep up beside him, he practically jogs up the staircase. "Miceli! Slow down," I say and can't help but chuckle. He's definitely a man on a mission. And that mission includes getting me naked and back in his bed. Although this time, he's definitely not going to keep his distance.

We reach his room and Miceli kicks the door shut, locking it. "I told Piero not to bother us." Hungry eyes slide down my body and I squeeze my hands together, my nerves kicking up to crazy heights.

"I should probably tell you—in case you haven't already guessed— that, um…" My voice trails off in embarrassment.

A muscle flexes in his cheek. "Are you a virgin, princess?"

I force a nod. "Surprise…" I say weakly.

His mouth edges up. "You're pretty adorable when you're not fighting me, you know that?"

"You're not disappointed?"

"Are you fucking kidding me? I'm thrilled." He advances on me, a predatory look in his dark eyes. "Knowing that I'm going to be the first man to touch you, to be inside of you…" He hisses out a breath, dropping a hand over the front of his pants. "I'm already hard."

My gaze drops and my cheeks flush.

"Alessia," Miceli murmurs, voice thick with desire. "Come here."

I take a few hesitant steps closer, until I'm standing directly in front of him.

"I'm going to take my time and make this so damn good for you."

"I'd appreciate that," I tell him honestly and his mouth lifts in a smile. He shrugs his suit jacket off, tossing it aside, and I watch, half mesmerized, as he begins unbuttoning his black dress shirt.

I'm wearing a light, flowy summer dress and not exactly ready to get naked yet in front of this man and his magnificent body. Especially in the bright light of day. All of a sudden, I'm wishing I liked to work out as much as I like to eat sweets.

Miceli slides his shirt off and I take a moment to soak in his firm chest and abs. Sheer perfection. My fingers itch to touch him. As if reading my thoughts, he steps closer, reaches for my hand and lays it on one of his spectacular pecs.

"Touch me, Alessia," he says, encouraging me. "Touch me wherever you want. I love your hands on my body."

My pulse skyrockets at the feel of his warm skin against my palm. He feels so hard, yet also smooth. I let my hand glide through the light dusting of hair on his chest and over to his other pec. He's so masculine and interesting. My hand drifts downward, fingers moving along the ridges of his tight abs, gliding through the grooves.

"How often do you work out?" I ask, and he chuckles.

"Monday through Friday. Do you approve?"

I nod, unable to find the words. My fingers brush over the trail of dark hair leading down into his pants and I freeze, not sure what to do.

"Don't be afraid to touch me," he rasps, hand covering mine. Then he guides it down past his belt buckle and over his hard cock surging against his zipper.

"Oh," I breathe, cupping his hardness. When I lightly squeeze, his nostrils flare and he drags my hand away.

"Enough."

"I thought you like me touching you."

"I do, but I can only handle so much. I promised you I'd take my time and that won't happen if you're doing that."

Before I can comment, Miceli reaches for the hem of my dress and lifts it straight up and over my head. Standing in front of him in only my bra and panties is nerve racking, especially when he's staring so intently at me.

"You're so beautiful," he murmurs, then pulls me into his arms. His mouth covers mine and I part my lips, welcoming him inside. His kisses are drugging and I melt against his chest, our tongues stroking and exploring. He tastes like the strawberry parfait we ate and I drink deeply, getting used to the feel of him pressed against me, kissing me so thoroughly.

There's denying the fact that I like it. A lot.

When Miceli finally breaks his mouth free, I'm panting. He lowers his face and begins kissing my neck while walking me backwards. The backs of my knees hit the bed and it takes me a moment to realize he's unsnapped my bra. It slides down my arms and he whips it off and aside. Taking a step back, Miceli soaks me in and then cups my breasts in his hands.

"So perfect," he whispers, kneading the flesh until I'm whimpering. "I'm going to kiss and lick and suck every inch of your body, princess. Starting with these tight little nipples."

The moment his mouth circles a nipple, I arch back, offering myself to him. He sucks, grazing his teeth over the sensitive bud, and I cry out. At the same time, he lowers me onto the bed and my back hits the mattress. My fingers twine through his hair as he continues kissing down to my stomach, swirling his tongue around my belly button and dipping it inside. When his fingers slide into the edges of my panties and he starts tugging them down, I tense slightly.

He's staring at my body again and this time I'm completely naked and exposed. And I'm not sure how I feel about it.

"Fuck, you're gorgeous, Alessia." With a growl, he unbuckles his belt, unzips his pants and they fall to the floor. Then he lowers himself down to his knees and drags his hands up my thighs, pushing my legs apart. "Show me that pretty pussy. Let me taste you."

My mouth drops open in shock at his dirty words—dirty words that have my pussy throbbing and wet. I can feel the wetness dripping from me and the moment Miceli's mouth touches my sensitive flesh, I cry out, arching up again. His tongue laps up my center then spears inside me, followed a moment later by his finger. It's the oddest sensation, but, oh my God, it feels good.

"Miceli," I rasp, twisting as he slides another finger into my soaked core. He pins my hips with one hand, thrusting two fingers inside me with the other and licking until I'm on the verge of screaming. And just when I think it can't get any more intense, his tongue circles my clit, teasing it unmercifully. After a torturous moment, he pulls it between his lips and sucks hard.

And everything inside of me explodes in a dazzling way that it never has before. Waves of pleasure ripple throughout my lower body and my hips buck up off the bed. I can't catch my breath and I feel my inner walls pulsing around his fingers.

"That's right. Don't fight it. Come for me." He starts kissing his way back up my body. "I love how wet you are for me. That soaking wet pussy is all mine and I'm going to fuck it so good, princess."

I'm a panting, whimpering mess and when he finally reaches my lips, he pauses. Instead of kissing them, he slides his fingers into my mouth and, for a shocked moment, I realize they're the same fingers that were just inside me. They're coated with my wetness and it tastes surprisingly sweet.

"See how good you taste," he murmurs wickedly.

Miceli removes his fingers then slides them into his mouth and licks my juices clean. I'm way too turned on by the dirtiness of it all to be disgusted and I reach out and brush my hand down the front of his fitted black boxer briefs. I want to see him in all his naked glory.

"You want my cock? Good because you're going to get it, sweet girl."

Biting down on my lip, needing more, needing his cock, I watch as he shoves his briefs off. My heart thunders as his huge erection bobs straight up. It's smooth and thick and long. There's moisture at the tip and I watch as he strokes himself several times. And somehow he seems to grow even bigger. To the point where I'm a little worried he might not fit.

Miceli pushes me back further onto the bed then settles himself between my legs. "Wrap your legs around my waist," he orders, voice harsh with need. I do as he says and the head of his swollen cock presses against my entrance. He must feel me tense because he kisses me slowly, dragging himself up and down my slit, and I relax slightly. Until he begins to enter me and it feels like he's tearing my body in two.

"Relax," he murmurs. "Drop your legs open and take my cock. It's your cock now, Alessia, and you're going to be a good girl and take every... last...inch."

Without warning, he thrusts hard and deep. I scream, burying my face against his chest, and my nails dig into the skin on his back. Miceli reaches down between our bodies, finds my clit and begins a rhythmic rubbing that has my thighs trembling and my pussy clenching. The pain fades and only a mild sting remains as he begins thrusting. Eventually, that goes away, too, and all I can feel is the way our bodies are moving together, one with each other. I'm stretched around him and he's moving hard and fast...so very deep...

My body starts shaking, muscles tightening, and the orgasm slams into me so hard, it knocks the breath from my lungs. My entire body trembles, pulsing deliciously, and I cry out Miceli's name as he continues to power into me.

If this is what married life to Miceli Rossi is going to be like, I'm absolutely fine with it. In fact, I welcome it.

10

MICELI

I'm powering into Alessia, my hips pistoning like fucking machinery, and I know I'm being to rough. But, I can't slow down and I can't pull back. Not when I feel like every atom in my body is about to explode into a million and one little pieces. I'm luck a man possessed. So, I do the only thing I can—I fuck my new wife into oblivion.

A body-spasming, mind-shattering release hits me with the strength of a rocket blasting into outer space. With a loud groan, I erupt, my hot seed shooting into Alessia's pulsing core. A dark, twisted part of me hopes she gets pregnant. Anything to keep her tied to me.

Dropping down, I kiss her passionately then pull out of her body and roll to the side. My hand drops on my chest and I'm breathing so damn hard. I savor the sting of Alessia's scratches on my back. There's so much I'm going to do to her; a thousand things I'm going to teach her.

Turning my head, I glance over to see her breathing has calmed down, but she still looks a little dazed. "Are you okay?" I ask.

"I think so," she murmurs softly.

Sitting up, I look over and see my seed leaking out of her sweet pussy. "I'll be right back," I tell her and slide off the bed. My feet pad across the room and I step into the bathroom where I wipe myself off. Then I grab a washcloth and run it under warm water. I've never cleaned a woman after sex. I guess I've rarely had intercourse without a condom either.

Hell, today has been a day of fucking firsts all around, I think, and head back over to my bed.

"Spread your legs, sweetness," I say and lower myself onto the bed.

"What?"

Instead of answering, I move the warm washcloth between her legs and gently wipe. "Are you sore?" I ask. Again, that twisted part of my brain hopes she is and that she can still feel my big cock deep inside her.

"Yes. A little."

Her voice is low, so quiet, and I have to strain to hear her. I finish cleaning her up and toss the washcloth. "Don't get all shy on me," I say, sliding closer, running my hand up her smooth side. With a squeal, she pulls sideways and I smirk. "Are you ticklish, princess?"

"No."

I run my fingers along her side again and she bursts into a fit of giggles. "Lying to me will only get you punished," I tell her then pull her closer and tickle the shit out of her. She cries out and squirms, kicking her legs, trying to escape. After a moment, I stop and she grabs the covers, pulling them up. I arch a brow. "You think that will stop me?"

"No, but…" Her voice trails off and her cheeks turn pink.

"But what?"

"I'm not used to sitting around naked in the middle of the day. And I usually wear pajamas to bed."

Crawling over, I try to pull the sheet away, but she holds tightly. For a moment, we have a little tug of war, but she's not going to win. I yank, exposing her nakedness, and she gasps.

"From now on, you sleep naked," I tell her. "Naked and ready for your husband." Then I lean down and capture her mouth in a deep kiss that makes it clear I won't tolerate anything else. I'm considering fucking her again even though I know I shouldn't so soon. She's probably more sore than she's admitting and I should give her time. I know I'm a large man. But the temptation is nearly overpowering.

"Miceli?" she whispers, looking up at me with big eyes the color of sea glass.

"What?" I murmur, brushing a lock of dark hair behind her ear.

"I need to call home. My mom and dad are probably going crazy with worry."

Even though I don't want to deal with her parents, I understand and know it's a necessary evil. Besides, that twisted part of me can't wait to see the look of defeat in Aldo's eyes after he discovers we're married. I've won. Alessia is mine and I've already filled her with my seed. With any luck, her belly will be round with my baby soon.

And there's not a damn thing Aldo DeLuca can do about it.

"Alright," I murmur, albeit reluctantly. "Get dressed and I'll take you there so we can talk to your parents. Then you can pack whatever you'd like to bring back here."

"Thank you."

However, I need to make one thing clear first. "Alessia, this is your home now. I know it's still new, but I want you to be comfortable. I'll keep you safe, protected and give you anything you need. All you have to do is ask. Okay?"

"Okay," she whispers.

"Good." After pressing a quick kiss to her lips, I roll off her before I change my mind and keep her in bed all day. But there's time for that tonight. After we visit her parents, explain the situation and gather her belongings, I'm whisking her straight back here and into my arms. And I don't plan on letting her leave this bedroom until tomorrow. Hell, maybe not. Maybe I'll keep her naked and writhing for another few days.

Alessia and I freshen up and get dressed, and then I have Leo drive us over to her parents' house. After what happened last night, I'm not stupid enough to go out alone. Besides, Leo is a good friend and having him by my side is always reassuring. Plus, his aim is outstanding and he can shoot a long-range bullseye with his eyes closed.

The closer we get to the DeLuca's brownstone, the more excited I become because I beat the old man at his own game. Barely twenty-four hours after smugly informing me that he wouldn't be calling me his son in law and having the audacity to wish me a nice life, I'm back, towing my prize beside me. His daughter is now my wife and has had my dick. Her virginity is non-existent and his plan to marry her off to Rocco Bianche is dead in the water. I thoroughly enjoy having the upperhand over people, especially ones who dare to fuck with me.

Once Leo pulls up outside the family home, Alessia tenses. Well, there's no way around the fact that this is going to be uncomfortable. "Let's go," I say and open my door. As I walk around the SUV to meet Alessia and take her hand, the front door of the brownstone flies open and I see Guilia.

"Alessia!" she cries. "Oh, thank God!"

Alessia releases my hand and runs up the steps to hug her mother. I don't like that she left me, but I get it. Apparently, they have a close relationship which might bode well for us and the bombshell we're about to drop on them. Well, if her mother speaks up, anyway.

As I walk up the stairs, Guilia sends me a curious look and turns to her daughter. "What's going on? Are you alright? Where have you been?"

"I'm fine," she assures her mother. "Can we go inside? We have some things to, ah, tell you."

Inwardly, I chuckle. That's a fucking understatement. I feel a little like the devil about to open a whole can of mischief. And, if I'm being honest, I'm loving every fucking second. The worst thing someone can do is tell me no because I will come back and upend his whole fucking world. And, in the end, I will have my way. So, really, there's no point denying me. Just say yes to me right away, every time. Otherwise, I can't be responsible for what happens. Well, I suppose I am responsible for stealing Alessia away, making her marry me and possibly impregnating her. But do I feel an ounce of guilt? Nope. I'd do the same exact same thing all over again without hesitation.

Rarely, if ever, do I feel remorse. I'm a man who makes a decision and stands by it.

"What the hell is going on?" Aldo exclaims, stalking into the foyer. "Why're you with this man, Alessia?"

This man? Really? My eyes narrow.

"Can we sit down and talk?" Alessia asks, avoiding the question. "Please."

I like to answer questions head-on, though, and if that means being blunt then so be it. "She's with me because she's now my wife," I tell them without preamble.

Guilia gasps and shock flashes across Aldo's face. After a brief moment, the shock morphs into a deadly look aimed straight at me. And, man, if looks could kill I'd be dead twice-over. I hold his angry gaze, refusing to break it. But, for whatever reason, I don't smirk or try to rub it in. I merely don't back down. Eventually, Aldo looks away and focuses on his daughter.

"Let's sit," he finally huffs out.

We walk into the formal living room and I follow Alessia over to the couch and drop down right next to her. It's clear I've claimed my woman and there's nothing anyone can say or do to change that. Reaching for her hand, I pull it over onto my upper thigh, threading my fingers through hers. Her parents' eyes drop, taking in the intimate gesture, and I feel Alessia stiffen slightly.

"Do you want to explain the situation or should I?" I ask her.

Alessia releases a low breath. "Me first," she says in a low voice then turns to face her parents. Her hand squeezes mine and I return the pressure, wanting her to know I'm here and support her. "There's no easy way to say this, but last night I ran away."

"You what?" her father practically roars.

"Calm down, Aldo," Guilia murmurs. "Let's listen to what they have to say."

"Since you weren't listening to me, I decided I had to leave and that it was time to live my own life and make my own decisions." Her voice drops. "I didn't want to be forced into a loveless marriage with a stranger."

"And isn't that exactly what has happened?" Aldo snaps, glaring at me. "Because I know you didn't go running to this man."

Annoyance prickles through me and I resist the urge to tell Aldo to go to hell. Instead, I bite my tongue and let Alessia handle it. I owe her that much. But, if she needs me to step in, I won't hesitate.

"No, I ran to the train station with every intention of leaving. Miceli followed me and we were talking out on the sidewalk when a man with a gun charged us and started shooting. Miceli saved my life."

Shocked silence fills the room. Finally, Aldo looks over at me. "Is this true?" he asks, face blank.

"Yes, sir," I respond, showing him respect and hoping for a truce. Because the truth is I don't want problems between our families. Ideally, it would be nice if we could all just get along.

"Who was this man?" Aldo asks.

"I think he was a hired thug, but I don't believe he was after me. He was going after Alessia."

Guilia gasps again and Aldo shakes his head, confused. "Why would anyone try to kill Alessia?" he asks, face screwing up in disbelief.

"I don't know," I admit. "But, I stopped him. Permanently." I don't normally kill men on the street in cold blood, but when you go after what's mine, I won't hesitate.

Aldo gives me a sharp nod. "Thank you for protecting her," he finally chokes out, and I nod back.

"Protecting her is my main concern. I brought her home with me and kept her safe. This morning, I married her. Offering her my name is the best protection I can give her and my house is a veritable fortress. You don't need to worry. I told you yesterday, I wanted to marry Alessia and we didn't see eye to eye. But, the deed is done and rest assured I have her best interests at heart. I promise to take good care of her."

"I appreciate that. And, I know you're a man of your word."

This meeting is going even better than I thought possible and, after pressing a kiss to Alessia's knuckles, I release her hand, stand up and offer my hand to her father. Aldo stands up and shakes my hand, albeit a bit reluctantly.

"Welcome to the family," he finally says.

There isn't much warmth in his eyes, but hopefully that'll change. One day. The good news is I have his blessing, even though it is a little on the tepid side. The even better news is Alessia will never have to deal with Rocco Bianche because she belongs to me now.

I wouldn't have it any other way. Because I am a man who is used to getting what he wants. And since the moment I met her, I've wanted Alessia. Now, she's mine.

11

ALESSIA

I suppose the visit to my parents' house goes better than I expect. My dad barely raised his voice and no one pulled a gun or got physical, so I'm going to count this as a win. Technically, I suppose there's nothing anyone can do at this point, anyway. Miceli has staked his claim, made me his wife and now I might be carrying his baby.

A shiver runs through me at the thought. How could so much have happened in the past twenty-four hours?

I don't exactly feel comfortable leaving Miceli alone with my parents, but I need to go pack some of my personal belongings upstairs. Plus, I'm hoping to talk to Gia alone and fill her in on the situation.

Once I reach my room, I start pulling open drawers and looking through my closet, throwing everything I want onto my bed. As I'm rummaging through the attached bathroom and packing essentials, I hear someone walk into the room and I turn to see my sister.

"What's going on?" she asks, standing in the doorway.

"Oh, I'm so glad you're here." I walk over, grab her arm and pull her into the bedroom. "We need to talk."

"Why is Miceli Rossi downstairs?"

I release Gia, clear my throat and spill it. "A lot happened yesterday and I don't want you to be upset."

"What happened?" she asks warily.

I immediately dive into the story, starting with how I snuck out and planned to run away. "I was outside of Penn Station when Miceli appeared out of nowhere. While we were talking, this man jumped out of a car and started shooting."

"What? Oh, my God."

"It was the scariest moment of my life. Miceli protected me, though, and drove me out of there and over to his place where he said I'd be safe."

"You?" She echoes, confused. "You don't think the gunman was after him?"

"He said he thinks I was the target."

Why didn't he bring you home?"

"Because he said I'd be safer with him. I'm not sure how to tell you this next part…"

"You spent the night with him."

It's not a question and I nod my head. "It's not like he gave me a choice. He's very bossy."

"Did you sleep with him?"

"Um…" I twist my hands in my lap then slowly nod. "But not until after…" My voice trails off. The last thing I want is for Gia to hate me and think I purposely stole her fiancé.

"After what?"

"After we were married."

Her eyes go wide in shock. "You married him?"

"Please, don't hate me! I know he was supposed to be your fiancé. But, Miceli kept saying I wasn't going to marry Rocco and he wasn't going to marry you. He told me his name would protect me and the next thing I know there's a priest and we're exchanging vows. It all happened so fast. Please, forgive me, Gia. I swear, I didn't mean for any of this to happen."

For a moment she doesn't say anything and I'm terrified I'm going to lose my big sister. Then, she sighs heavily. "I don't hate you, Lessi. I love you and I want you to be happy. Does Miceli make you happy?"

I consider her question and know it's too early to be able to answer that question honestly. "I barely know him," I admit. "But, there's something there. Even though he's a little scary, he also has this sweet side. I think he likes taking care of me."

Gia smiles. "Then I'm happy for you."

"You promise? Because I didn't plan on any of this and—"

"I promise." She grabs my hands in hers and squeezes. "I told you yesterday that man was smitten by you. And this merely proves it. We would've made a terrible match, anyway. Especially since I could tell how much he liked you."

"I love you, Gia," I say softly.

"Love you, too, Lessi."

After we hug it out, Gia helps me pack my stuff up into a big suitcase. I'm about to drag it downstairs when Miceli appears and takes it from me.

"I've got it," he states. He looks over at Gia, nods and has the decency to appear slightly uncomfortable.

"You better take good care of my sister," Gia says.

"I will," he promises.

"Good. Otherwise I'll hunt you down and steal her back home."

Miceli reaches for my hand and tugs me closer. "I'll treat her like a princess," he murmurs and kisses my temple. Of course, I blush to my roots.

After saying goodbye to Gia and my parents, Miceli loads my suitcase up in the back of his car and we get inside. "That went better than expected," he says, and I nod as Leo pulls away from the curb.

"It really did." I sneak a glance over at Miceli's strong profile. I still can't believe this man is my husband. The entire situation is still throwing me for a loop and I honestly don't know if I'll adjust any time soon.

"Gia seems fine with it."

"Despite what she said, I don't think she wanted to get married. No offense to you, but she's probably a little relieved."

Miceli turns to face me. "Everything worked out exactly as it should have." His dark eyes search mine. "You're right where you should be—with me. And if you need anything, let me know."

"Okay," I murmur. "I'd like to see my best friend Cara. I have to call her and tell her where I am."

"I'd like to meet her. Invite her over for lunch or dinner."

"Really?" Even though Miceli has a ruthless reputation when it comes to business, I'm seeing a different side to the mafia kingpin. A gentle, kind, caring side that makes me like him a lot. "Okay, thank you."

Just when I'm about to ask him if tonight is okay, his phone rings. Miceli switches right back into brutal business mode and gives a few, quick answers. His tone is brusque, almost annoyed, and he keeps the conversation short and clipped. After he disconnects the call, he frowns.

"Something has come up and I need to attend a meeting with the Five Families." His gaze meets Leo's in the rear view mirror. "L, I want you to take Alessia home and stay with her. Keep an eye on things."

"You don't want me to go with you?" he asks.

I can hear the surprise in his voice.

"No. Watch Alessia and keep her safe."

"What about you?" I ask.

"What about me, princess?"

"Who's going to keep you safe?"

His mouth edges up. "I can take care of myself. But thanks for the concern." He reaches over and lays his hand on my thigh, gently squeezing.

I nod and when we reach the safety of the underground garage, Miceli pulls me into his arms and kisses me very thoroughly right in front of Leo. At first, I'm embarrassed then I'm swooning. Good God, Miceli Rossi can kiss me senseless. When he finally breaks away, I feel a little dizzy and weak in the knees.

"Be good for Leo, okay? And I'll be home in time for dinner."

"Okay." As he starts to walk away, I call out, "You be careful, too."

Miceli looks back over his shoulder and a strange look crosses over his handsome face. "I will," he murmurs, and I instantly wonder if anyone else has ever shown any true concern or care for his safety before. I get the feeling if anyone has before, it wasn't a woman he was seeing.

Leo guides me straight over to the elevator, wheeling my suitcase, and, right before I step inside, I turn and see Miceli standing by his car, watching and making sure we get inside okay. The man takes the role of protector to a whole new level. But, it makes me feel good knowing he cares about my well-being. My father has always watched out for us, but not quite like this. It seems that Miceli is an extreme person and puts one-hundred and ten percent into everything he does, no matter what that is. I can still feel a twinge between my legs from where his extremely large and very demanding cock was earlier. Yeah, he gives everything his all whether it's business or sex.

As the elevator takes us up to the 129th floor, I study Leo. It's a good name for him since he resembles a lion. His chest is broad and stretches his t-shirt to the point it looks a little too tight. The sleeves appear to dig into his upper arm muscles and, currently, his big arms are crossed in front of him. His long, light brown hair has golden highlights and is pulled back into a loose man bun, and a dark scruff covers his lower face. Unlike Miceli who is always so polished-looking and neatly-dressed in a suit, Leo appears more laid back and casual in his jeans and t-shirt.

When the door finally glides open, Leo motions for me to step out first. It's so quiet in the beautiful, bright apartment and it occurs to me that I have the entire place to myself right now. Well, except for Leo, but he probably has things to do. I'm so curious about my new husband and I decide to explore. After all, he told me this is my home too now and that he wants me to be comfortable. As I'm debating where to go first, Leo tells me he's going to take my suitcase up to the bedroom.

"Thank you," I tell him, watching as he heads that way. Once he's out of sight, I wander down the hallway and peek into every room. When I reach what must be Miceli's office, I step inside and instantly get a whiff of his scent hanging in the air. He has this incredibly sexy smell that is very masculine. I'm not sure what it is, but it has notes of citrus and leather. And, of course, it makes my stomach somersault.

I don't think I've ever been this curious about another person before and I'm drawn over to his large, wooden desk and look down to see what's on it. It's very neat and well-organized, not a thing out of place. Other than his laptop and an empty coaster, there's not a speck of dust and the dark wood shines as though it were just dusted. There's also a framed photo and I reach over and pick it up. Leaning a hip against the desk, I study the picture behind the glass, and come to the conclusion it must be Miceli and his family.

Squinting, I study each man, the young woman and the older couple. They're all smiling and it looks like there's a poinsettia on the nearby table. I'm assuming it's his family at Christmas. His brothers are just as good-looking as Miceli, but a little younger and don't appear quite as formidable. The woman must be his sister and she's stunningly beautiful.

When a throat clears, my head snaps up and I quickly set the picture down where I found it, feeling guilty for being caught snooping. Leo watches me closely.

"Can I help you find anything?" he asks.

"Uh, no. I was just looking around."

"Mmhmm."

Moving away from the desk, I walk over to the window and look out at the amazing view of the city. I don't hear Leo leave, so I glance over my shoulder to see him still standing there. *Dammit.* I hope he isn't planning to follow me around everywhere.

"It's a lovely view," I say, trying to break the awkward moment.

"Mmhmm."

Turning back around, I decide to go upstairs and unpack my things. And Leo follows me. Once we reach the master suite, he remains in the sitting room and I go into the bedroom. At least he didn't come into the bedroom, too. I have a weird feeling he'd follow me straight into the bathroom if I let him. The men around here really take their protector role to new levels of extreme.

I pull the door shut a little so I can have some privacy. I didn't bring a lot of things with me, but enough to keep me busy for the next forty minutes or so as I organize and put things away. When I'm finished, I look around and wonder what to do next. I'm itching to look through Miceli's things, but with Leo right in the next room, I don't want him reporting back that I was being a nosy snoop. I suppose I could lay down and take a nap, but I'm not tired. Drumming my fingers against my thighs, I realize what I really want is information about the man I married.

And, if Leo is going to be my shadow, maybe I can pry some intel from him. After all, they're about the same age and they seem like friends more so than business associates. Unfortunately, Leo has proved he isn't the most chatty bodyguard.

With a plan forming, I walk out of the bedroom and see him slouched down in a chair, ankle crossed over his knee, and scrolling through his phone. The moment I appear, he snaps upright, setting the phone on his large thigh.

"Are you going to follow me everywhere?" I ask.

"Pretty much."

"Then you should know I'm going down to the kitchen," I tell him and sashay past. As expected, he follows on my heels all the way down to the sun-soaked kitchen. It smells clean, like lemons, and the marble surfaces gleam. Miceli must have a cleaning crew that comes in and keeps the place spotless because not one thing is out of place or even remotely dirty or unkempt-looking. I wonder if he's OCD and has an aversion to clutter and germs or if he's just a neat freak? I decide to ask my new shadow who is now sitting at the kitchen table.

"Does a cleaning company come here?" I ask, running a finger along the sparkling surface of the island. Above me, there's a rack full of hanging pots and pans with not even a speck of dust on them.

"Three times a week," he informs me.

"Is Miceli a neat freak and weird about things being organized and shiny?"

Leo chokes back a laugh and I look over. "He likes things to be in order," he finally manages to say.

"Clearly." I start opening drawers, searching for the things I'm going to need. Since Leo is fairly closed-mouthed and I want information, I'm going to rely on some advice I heard a while back—that there are two ways to get to a man: sex or food. Sex is off the table, so I'm going to try baking my world-class lasagna. It's an old family recipe with a little extra goodness to it that makes most mouths water. Also, I'm going to make some dessert in the form of the most delicious chocolate cookies known to man and I plan on having Leo taste test them. Besides, when Miceli comes home, I want to have dinner ready for him.

After searching through the pantry and cupboards, I luckily find all the ingredients I need. I think someone must grocery shop and cook, too, and then I remember Piero.

"Where's Piero?" I ask.

"It's his day off."

"What does Miceli do without him? Can he cook?"

That gets me a belly laugh. "No. Miceli can't cook to save his life."

"Lucky for him, I'm pretty good in the kitchen." As I start mixing ingredients, I notice Leo's nose perk up.

"What're you making?" he finally asks, watching as I blend butter, sugar and eggs.

"My family lasagna and chocolate chip cookies for dessert." I slant him a look. "I don't suppose you'd like to be my taste-tester?"

He sits up straighter. "I can do that."

Smothering a smirk, I move around the kitchen and work on the meal and dessert. I keep him engaged in small talk, warming him up with a spoonful of chocolate chip cookie batter. "How is it?" I ask, and he groans.

"Delicious."

"Good." While dropping spoonfuls of batter on the baking tray, Leo watches closely, practically drooling. "So, how did you and Miceli meet?" I ask.

"School."

"How old were you?"

"Ten maybe?"

I place the tray into the oven and set the timer. Then, I walk back over to the island and continue working on the lasagna. Deciding to cut to the chase, I say, "Do you give more than one or two word answers because I'm very curious about the man I married and if you want some of this absolutely delicious food I'm making, I'm going to need more from you."

Leo tilts his head, studying me. "I think I like you," he announces.

"Okaaay," I say slowly, but inwardly I'm smiling. *Food will get a man every single time,* I think triumphantly.

Leo stands up, moves closer, and sits down on the opposite side of the island from me. "Miceli needs someone like you in his life."

"Someone like me?"

"He needs…" He frowns as though searching for the right word. "Softness."

Well, he is rather hard, I think wickedly, but I don't dare say that out loud. "He seems very focused on work."

"He is. It's his responsibility to make sure the Rossi name stays on top and remains one to be feared. That doesn't come easy."

"No, I imagine it doesn't." I know my husband is a force to be reckoned with and I can only imagine what he'd done to keep his family on top. Their reputation is daunting. "Have you always been his bodyguard?"

"No. I worked for a different family at one point." His voice trails off and, I swear, a note of regret, or maybe it's sadness, creeps into his voice. "But, that was a long time ago. Anyway, I've been his personal guard for the past five years."

Even though Leo isn't a big talker, he's starting to warm up to me and that makes me happy. Eventually, it doesn't feel like I'm pulling teeth and he begins offering a little information here and there on his own. I find out a few new things about my husband, but mostly that he's under constant pressure with the Five Families and he works way too hard.

After Leo gobbles down three cookies, he eyes me closely. "I think you might turn out to be a good thing. I have to admit, I had my doubts at first."

"And now you're convinced?" I ask teasingly.

"Not convinced," he admits shrewdly, "but Miceli already seems...I don't know. Happier...lighter."

Hearing his friend say that pleases me more than I thought possible. "Good," I say softly. "I'm glad."

And, I really am. There's so much darkness in Miceli's world and being his light is something I know I can do. In fact, it's something I really, really want to do.

12

MICELI

Sitting at the large, round table, I face the heads of the other four mafia families of New York City—The Bianchi's, The DeLuca's, The Caparelli's and The Milano's. We're the ones in charge, the select few who run everything. Because of the agreement made between our great grandfathers years ago, we haven't shed each other's blood. But, right now, the temptation to do so is nearly my undoing. Starting with that rat bastard Rocco Bianche.

Trying to ignore the elevated tension and side eyes I'm getting, I finally blow. "Just fucking speak up!" I yell and slam my fist against the table.

"You shouldn't have forced Alessia DeLucca to marry you," Rocco Bianche snaps. "She was mine and you fucking stole her from me."

I finally turn my full attention to Rocco and squeeze my hands into tight fists, willing my skyrocketing blood pressure to go down. "First, her name is now Alessia Rossi and don't you forget it. Second, she's mine and I don't give a shit whether you like it or not."

"She wasn't yours! Alessia was promised to me!"

"Maybe yesterday, but promises were broken and now she's mine."

"Take it easy," the head of the Caparelli family orders. He's older, but I wouldn't say wiser. With a head of shocking white hair and a tendency to order his enemies killed execution-style and without so much as a conversation first, I glance over at him. We are normally on the same page, but right now I wait with baited breath to see if that's true or not. "Give it up, Rocco. Miceli laid claim before you and, knowing him, the girl probably already has a babe in her belly."

I toss a smug smile over to Rocco who glares back at me. But, since Aldo DeLuca is sitting beside me, I don't rub that fact in or be vulgar about it. Instead, I simply say, "It's a possibility."

"Move on, Bianche," the head of the Milano family says, agreeing with us as well. "Why would you want Rossi's leftovers, anyway?" The fifty-some year old, balding man slants an apologetic look toward Aldo. "Sorry, but she's Miceli's now."

"Enough talk about my daughter," Aldo finally says. "What's done is done. Is it how I planned? No. Do I have to be happy about it? No. But there's nothing left to be done about it. Nothing except apologize to you Rocco and accept Miceli as my new son-in-law."

"I don't want apologies," Rocco gripes. "I wanted that virgin's blood."

"Too fucking bad," I growl, my nails digging into my palms.

"Enough!" Aldo roars. For a moment, no one says anything. Then Aldo pulls in a deep, steadying breath. "However, in order to make up for what happened, Rocco, I'd like to offer my older daughter Gia's hand in marriage."

My attention snaps over to Aldo. Even though I don't agree with his decision to use Gia as a sacrificial lamb, I keep my mouth shut. For now, anyway. But, I already know my Alessia isn't going to be happy about the situation. Especially since we can all agree on the fact that Rocco is a lying sack of shit who most likely killed his last significant other. *What the hell is Aldo thinking?* I wonder. And why is he so desperate to remain in the Bianche family's good graces?

"I'll consider the offer," Rocco says, not looking happy at all. "Even though Gia was never my first choice."

"You should consider yourself lucky to have my oldest daughter," Aldo says, eyes narrowing and voice steely. But, Rocco clams up fast and doesn't say another word. The idiot knows he's pissed DeLuca off and I'm glad. Hopefully, I can get into his good graces at some point.

"What you did was a shit, sneaky thing, Rossi," Milano states, looking at me, and I send him an unconcerned glance, raising my middle finger.

"I took what I wanted and I have zero regrets." I look from each family head to the next, refusing to apologize or back down. "And if anyone would like to continue challenging me about my wedding and new wife, things are going to get really ugly really goddamn fast."

None of us is allowed to have a weapon in the meeting room, but I have my fists balled and right now I'm damn close to swinging them into someone's face and doing serious damage. The tenuous peace we somehow manage to maintain all these years seems to be fraying a little more every day. Truthfully, I can't imagine it's going to last much longer.

"There are other things to discuss during this meeting," Caparelli says, looking around the table. "Rossi, I wish you and your new wife a happy future."

"Thank you." The others mumble their good wishes. Well, everyone except Bianche, but I'm hardly surprised. "I think we need to discuss what happened the other night."

"And what are you referring to?" Milano asks.

"Alessia and I were almost gunned down outside of Penn Station." I tell everyone the story of what happened and shocked gasps fill the room. I study each man closely and either they're all completely unaware of what happened or someone is putting on an Academy Award winning performance.

Aldo DeLucca looks sick to his stomach, knowing he almost lost his youngest daughter, and the others appear genuinely upset. Surprisingly, Rocco, too. Everyone starts talking at once, trying to glean more information about what happened. I tell them everything I know—which isn't much—and ask for their support in tracking down this new enemy.

"If someone is targeting Rossi, he may as well be targeting all of us," Caparelli states. Our fathers are close and I'm glad he's always been the first to have my back.

"And if one of us is taken out, who will be next?" Milano adds. "We all know our enemies are everywhere and chomping at the bit to destroy us and to usurp our control over this city."

"We need to work together and protect each other," DeLucca says. "It's in all of our best interests."

Even though these men have the power to push my buttons, I couldn't agree more. "Together, we're stronger," I state, looking over at Bianche whose face is blank.

"Yes," Rocco says, nodding his head. "And maintaining our Italian stronghold is key."

Finally, I think we're all on the same page again. At least, for today. But, what I don't say is if a single hair on my new wife's head is touched, I will wipe out the perpetrator's entire bloodline. Without a second thought and with zero remorse.

After the meeting goes too long, I can't wait to get back home. I drive way too fast, park my car and hurry up to the apartment. The truth is, I missed my little wife. Ever since the moment I left her to attend the meeting, I haven't been able to stop thinking about her. It's like she's ingrained herself into my brain and she's always there, right at the edge of my thoughts.

When I step off the elevator, I immediately smell all sorts of deliciousness and the first thing I hear is Alessia's tinkle of sweet laughter. Thinking she may have invited her friend Cara over, I start toward the kitchen then abruptly stop short when I hear more, deeper laughter. I stiffen when I recognize Leo's happy rumble.

A strange wave of jealousy hits me and I walk over to the kitchen, stand in the archway and stare at the scene before me. Leo and Alessia are sitting at the island, a heaping plate of cookies between them, talking and dipping them in glasses of milk. I'm not sure whether to be angry or happy that they're getting along so well. But there's no denying the fact that I'm annoyed. It should be me sitting there with her. That beautiful, sunshiny smile should be directed at me, not him. Forcing back a growl, I continue to watch their interaction a couple moments more. But then Leo senses my presence and turns. But, he doesn't look guilty or anything. Instead, he motions for me to come join them, a big smile on his face.

"Hey, Miceli. Holy hell, you've gotta try these cookies."

He's not trying to steal your wife, I tell myself and walk over to join them. *He's your best friend.* I don't know why I instantly turn irrational when it comes to Alessia, but I do. To the point where it's starting to concern me. She unsettles me, makes me do and think crazy thoughts I wouldn't normally.

"Hi," she says shyly as I move up beside her. "I made lasagna for dinner."

"It smells really good," I say.

"The table is already set. I invited Leo to join us, but he says he can't."

"Nope, got things to do," Leo announces, standing up and sending me a discreet wink. "Have fun tonight." He slaps me on the back and heads toward the door.

"Oh, don't forget your cookies!" Alessia calls out.

I reach for the tupperware and toss the container to Leo. "Thanks," he says, catching it. "I would've been so pissed if I'd forgotten these. Best fucking cookies I've ever had."

My friend walks out and I turn to Alessia. "Looks like you charmed Leo," I say, studying her reaction.

"Not me," she states with a smile. "It was the chocolate chip cookies."

My mouth edges up. "So, you made dinner?"

She nods. "I figured it would be the wifely thing to do. There's home-made lasagna from my secret family recipe, fresh tossed salad with a vinaigrette, garlic bread and cookies for dessert."

"Wow, you've been busy." I don't ask, but I wonder if she missed me as much as I missed her.

"C'mon, everything is waiting in the dining room."

We head into the small, formal dining area and I see the table is already set and I reach for the bottle of wine, opening it. After pouring us each a glass, I lift mine and clink it against hers. "Thank you for this. It was very thoughtful, and it all looks and smells delicious."

"Well, let's hope you like it after you eat it," she jokes.

"If it's half as good as it smells then rest assured I will."

After my plate is full, I take a big bite of lasagna and moan. "Damn, Alessia. This is so good."

Alessia shifts in her seat and smiles. "I'm glad you like it."

"I don't like it, I love it."

My compliment makes her cheeks turn a petal-pink. "How did your meeting go?" she asks.

I hesitate, not wanting to get into it or tell her yet about her father offering Gia's hand to Rocco for marriage. "It could've gone better," I say vaguely. "But, let's talk about you. How was your afternoon?"

"Good! I spent most of it cooking and talking to Leo. It took a minute to crack him, but once he gets talking, he certainly has a lot to say."

"Does he?" I arch a brow, suddenly wanting to wring Leo's neck.

"He loves you like a brother, you know, and would do anything for you."

Shit. Okay, so I would never actually hurt Leo and guilt pierces through me. "He is like a brother."

"He said you two go pretty far back," she says, and I nod, biting into a piece of the lightest, crustiest bread I've ever tasted. So good. "I'm glad he has your back."

"And I have his." But, that doesn't mean I share. So, as much as I love Leo, he better treat Alessia like a long-lost sister. "But, if he ever crosses the line...does anything inappropriate..."

"What exactly are you inferring?"

That tart tone is back in her voice and I narrow my eyes, dropping my fork on the plate with a resounding clatter. "Do you need to ask? Because if you don't know then I'd be happy to explain."

Pushing my chair back, I stand up and round the table. Crazy, possessive jealousy washes over me and I can't help it, much less control it. I'm growing obsessive over my wife and I reach down, tipping Alessia's chin up so she's looking up at me.

"Make no mistake about it. You are my wife and I won't tolerate unfaithfulness."

"Nor will I from you," she responds, blue-green eyes snapping fire.

"Good. I'm glad we're on the same page. And, if any man, Leo included, ever touches you or talks to you or even looks at you with lust or desire, you will tell me so I can take care of it."

Alessia pulls her chin away from my hand and laughs. Fucking laughs.

"And what will you do?" she asks, not taking my threat seriously.

"I'll kill him," I state without blinking.

She instantly sobers and realizes I'm not joking. "You're serious, aren't you?"

"As a heart attack."

Alessia studies me closely then lays a hand on the lapel of my suit jacket. "I don't want you to kill anyone else for me," she whispers. "And I promise to be a faithful wife as long as you're a faithful husband."

Her words stoke a fire in my belly, and I lean down and capture her lips in a hard, demanding kiss. The need to punish her for having such a perfectly lovely afternoon without me—with Leo—has me scooping her up out of her chair, shoving the dishes and plates aside, and setting her ass on the edge of the table.

"Miceli," she gasps when I start tugging her leggings down.

"I need you. Now."

"But—"

The word is smothered against her lips as I kiss the ever-loving shit out of and rip her panties off.

Time for dessert.

13

ALESSIA

With a cry, I fall back on the dining room table and Miceli moves between my legs, pushing them further apart with his big thighs, and kissing me like he's desperate and can't seem to get enough.

He's stripped me from the waist down and I only feel exposed for a moment because then he's covering me with his body. I'm not sure what put him in this voracious mood, but I have a feeling my afternoon with Leo may have something to do with it. It's hard to believe this attractive, very virile, alpha man is...jealous. It's the only explanation for his behavior.

And now he's staking his claim and marking me thoroughly as his. A part of me enjoys knowing I have that kind of power over him. It makes me think he might actually care. Or, maybe I'm just being delusional and it's only about sex for him.

My eyes open when he suddenly pulls back and I watch him rip off his suit jacket and loosen his tie. He doesn't bother removing it...or his shirt. His long fingers move down, fumbling with his belt, followed by the button on his pants and zipper. So many clothes. I can't help but smirk because he's so frantic to kick his pants off.

After tugging his pants and boxer briefs down, his gaze meets mine for a brief moment before he drops down between my spread legs. That luscious mouth of his latches onto my pussy and I cry out. He's not holding back and it feels like he's eating me alive with his tongue, lips and teeth. When his fingers get involved, two of them sliding deep and thrusting in and out, I writhe, trying to squeeze my thighs together.

My body begins to tighten and I can feel my release hovering just out of reach. I'm almost there, but not quite. Not until he sucks my clit into his mouth, teasing it with his tongue. Everything snaps and I grab his hair, pulling hard as the orgasm blasts me into the stratosphere.

Somehow, this man knows how to work my body just right. Lying on the table, I'm a shaking mess and panting hard as aftershocks ripple through my body.

"Best dessert I ever had," he rasps, licking his lips. Then he stands, spreading my slickness over his cock and begins roughly stroking it.

I let out a breath, my chest still heaving, unable to pull my eyes off what he's doing. How he's making his already huge cock grow longer and thicker. And how he's spreading my wetness all over himself.

"You like watching?" he asks, voice harsh with need.

The words are caught in my throat and my pussy throbs at his words. At the way he's choking his enormous cock.

"Tell me you like looking at me, princess."

I'm breathing so hard and I can't seem to look away. Precum spills from the engorged tip and he grabs my hand, dragging it over, covering mine with his as he continues running his hand up and down his hard length.

"Touch me. Squeeze me," he encourages, tightening his hand around mine, showing me exactly what he likes. "That's right, sweet girl. Harder."

His head falls back and he releases a desperate, needy rasp from deep within his throat. Then he abruptly releases my hand, grasps my hips and drags me forward. My ass is hanging off the edge of the table and Miceli slams into me with one powerful stroke. My body arches up and a cry tears from my lips as he thrusts hard, in and out. The dishes and silverware on the table shake and rattle with every movement, and I grab his tie, pulling hard, and wrap my legs around his lean hips.

"Take it," he hisses. "Take your husband deeper."

A whimper fills the air and I realize it's me. I lift my hips, meeting his strokes, and trying to take even more of his length. Just like he wants. He's pounding into my slick core and I turn my head, eyes on the wine sloshing around in my glass. Just when I think there's no way I'll orgasm again so soon, his fingers find my clit and begin to massage and roll the swollen nub.

"Miceli," I gasp as my inner muscles begin to tighten once again, squeezing around his cock, somehow managing to draw him as deep as possible. Our eyes lock for a brief, intense moment before mine roll back in my head and I scream from the intense pleasure which slams into me. Miceli immediately follows, his entire body consumed by a shudder as he erupts.

The heat of his release fills me and I sigh softly, out of breath and completely spent. Unable to move, I feel Miceli pull out and push me further back onto the table. A napkin gently wipes between my thighs then he scoops me up into his arms.

"Let's go upstairs," he murmurs, pressing a kiss to my temple.

"What about the dishes?" I ask, knowing we should clean up first.

"Fuck the dishes. They aren't going anywhere."

Neither am I, I think. It scares me to know that I'm softening toward this man. I should hate him for forcing me into marriage, but I can't. He intrigues me, protects me and gives me the greatest pleasure I've ever known.

Still though, I may have given him my body, but I'm keeping my heart locked up tight. I know he's doing the same thing, too. Fucking is one thing. Involving emotions and opening myself up to love is a completely different and terrifying thing. Because if I fall in love with Miceli, he'll have the power to break me. I saw firsthand what happened to my sister when she took a chance and fell in love. Poor Gia is a shell of her former self, broken beyond repair. And that's a fate I'd like to avoid.

Miceli keeps me awake most of the night and teaches me things I never even knew existed. Sexual positions I didn't think were possible. It turns out, I'm way more flexible than I ever thought and, by the time morning comes, I'm exhausted and sore in so many places. It's extremely clear that my new husband is an insatiable beast who loves sex.

Sitting up in bed, I drop the sheet and stretch my arms up over my head. I'm getting used to being naked, but it's not like I have a choice in the matter. Miceli likes my clothes off and being skin to skin with me. I have to admit, I like it, too. A lot.

I reach my hand over and lay it on Miceli's side of the bed. The sheets are cool which tells me he got up a while ago and let me sleep in. Well, he should since he kept waking me up with his fingers, his mouth and his cock. Not that I'm complaining. It just takes a little getting used to.

I'm debating whether it's safe to hop into the shower without getting jumped when Miceli strides into the room, a very relaxed and satisfied look on his gorgeous face.

"Good morning, princess," he says and leans down to kiss me. His hand grips the side of my neck and jawline firmly and his tongue slides into my mouth. With a disapproving sound, I pull back and cover my mouth.

"I haven't brushed my teeth yet."

He chuckles. "And? You think you taste any less sweet? Because you don't."

"Morning breath is the worst," I insist, scooting off the bed, dragging the sheet with me. Even though I was just thinking I'm more comfortable being naked, I realize that's only in the dark and at night. Not in broad daylight with the sun shining in and highlighting every one of my flaws.

But, being the troublemaker he is, Miceli steps on the edge of the sheet, halting my steps.

"Hey!" I try tugging it free, but it doesn't budge. "Can I please have my sheet?"

"No."

"Miceli—"

"You have two options. Either walk to that bathroom naked, slowly, and let me watch. Or, I'll be following you straight in there and joining you in the shower."

My eyes widen and I can't miss those wicked dimples of his on full display. That's one thing we haven't done yet and I really enjoy my alone-time while I'm bathing. I've told him that and I think it's the only reason why we haven't had sex in the shower yet. But, I'm not sure how much longer I can hold him off. There's a feral light glowing in his eyes and I quickly let go of the sheet and spin around, getting ready to run.

"Slowly," he reminds me and I force myself to sashay to the bathroom slower than normal.

When I reach the door and glance over my shoulder, I immediately notice his hungry look and the huge bulge tenting his pants. How can he possibly want to have sex again? With a shake of my head, I quickly close the door. But not before I hear another low chuckle.

"You can run, princess, but you can't hide. Not from me," he says through the door.

My heart pounds wildly and I pause as I reach for my toothbrush, wondering if he's going to come in here. After a few seconds, I let out a slow breath.

"Brunch is set up downstairs," he tells me. "Come join me when you're ready."

"Okay."

He must realize how sore I am because he lets off the hook and I hear him walk away. It occurs to me that I must be pregnant by now. He's never bothered with protection, and I'm certainly not on birth control. After all the ways and times he's taken me, how can I not be? My hand drops, covering my flat stomach. I'm not sure how I feel about it. About any of this. It's still all so new and strange. My entire life was flipped upside down in such a short amount of time.

As I brush my teeth, I decide that I want to get to know Miceli better, but outside of the bedroom. I'm getting to know him extremely well when it comes to what he likes, how he wants to be touched and what makes him groan loudest. But, I want to get to know and understand the man behind the curtain. The one he doesn't show anyone else. I think the best way to start is to meet his family. I also need to call Cara and invite her over. We've texted, of course, and she knows what's happened, but I need my best friend to come over so we can catch up in person.

After a quick shower, I wander downstairs and meet Miceli in the kitchen. The moment I pass the dining room, my attention zeroes in on the table and I blush furiously. Swallowing hard, I try not to think about the things we did on that surface where we eat.

Stepping into the kitchen, I see a delicious-looking spread of food on the table. From fresh fruit parfaits to pastries to waffles and coffee. "Mmm," I murmur, sniffing the air. "It smells like Piero was baking."

As if on cue, Piero walks over and sets a warm coffee cake on the table. "Fresh out of the oven, Mrs. Rossi. I hope you like cinnamon."

"I love it. Thank you, Piero, this all looks wonderful."

He smiles widely and I sit down, glancing over at Miceli who is studying me closely, a newspaper in his hands. Before he can say anything, I reach for a strawberry parfait and say, "I'd like to meet your family. When can we visit them?"

A thick, dark brow arches up and he snaps the paper shut, setting it aside. "They're all over the place and very busy," he responds.

I frown as Piero slices a piece of coffee cake and sets it on a plate. It feels like Miceli just brushed my request aside, but I'm not letting it go so easily.

"You know, they're my family now, too. And I'd really like to get to know them."

"I already told you my parents live in Sicily and rarely visit the States. And my siblings—" His phone vibrates with a text and he picks it up and frowns. Letting out a long, low, resigned breath, he looks up and meets my curious gaze. "Well, you're about to get your wish, princess, because my brother just texted me. He's on his way up."

"Which brother?" I ask, growing excited.

"Vin."

"It's Vincentius, right?"

Miceli nods and stands up. "C'mon. Let's see what he wants."

I hurry after Miceli whose long-legged stride is hard to keep up with. But, I'm really looking forward to meeting his brother. So, of course, we're both shocked when the elevator door opens and a whole slew of good-looking, dark-haired people exit.

"Mom? Dad?" Surprise flits over Miceli's face.

"We heard you got married," a man with salt and pepper hair announces in a thick Italian accent. "Why did I have to find out through Caparelli?"

"You're all here?" he asks, sounding amazed. "I thought you were flitting around Europe." He directs the statement to one of his brothers and a quick look reveals the Rossi family has damn good genes.

"Are you going to introduce us to your new wife or what?" the attractive, older woman asks, hands going on her round hips.

"Everyone, this is Alessia," Miceli announces. "Alessia, these are my parents, Salvatore and Carmela. And my brothers, Vin, Enzo and Angelo. And, my baby sister, Carlotta."

They all start talking at once and I'm pulled into hugs from every which way. Their boisterous energy and loud enthusiasm is contagious and I'm smiling from ear to ear. As scary as Miceli can sometimes be, his family is friendly and welcoming. And, I instantly adore them.

"You can call me Lottie. Everyone does, but I don't mind at all," his sister says, reaching for my arm and dragging me toward the living room. "Oh, my God, let me see that rock."

As Carlotta checks out my ring which now fits my finger perfectly after being sized, I glance back at Miceli with a helpless chuckle and he shrugs.

Once we're all seated, I look around, a bit overwhelmed. They're all staring at me, just as curious about me as I am about them. And, oh my, they're a good-looking group. Miceli wedges his way in between me and one of his brothers.

"Move over, Ang," he orders, sitting down beside me.

"Still see you're as bossy as ever," Angelo comments with a wide grin.

"You know it. Now move your ass over so I can sit beside my wife."

Angelo laughs and slides down, making room. Miceli reaches for my hand and I hold on tightly. I know I said I wanted to meet his family, and I'm glad this is happening, but it's all just a bit overwhelming.

"Tell us exactly how you wound up with Alessia and not Gia," Salvatore states, cutting right to the chase. I can see where Miceli gets his firm, bossy tone from and I look over at his father who looks to be in his mid-50's and is still very fit and handsome.

"Alessia and I met first," Miceli says smoothly. "And I knew she was the one for me."

"Oh, that's so romantic," Carlotta exclaims. "Sounds like love at first sight."

Neither of us comments and I think we both tense up a little.

"Don't be ridiculous, Lottie," Enzo scoffs. "There's no such thing as love at first sight. Now, lust at first sight, sure."

Carlotta smacks her brother's arm. "Just because you've never been in love doesn't mean it can't happen."

"Excuse me, but—"

"Enzo is in love with himself," Angelo says and everyone cracks up. "Does that count?"

"Look who's talking," Enzo responds easily, a gleam in his dark brown eyes. "Ang, don't you have a mirror above your bed?"

Angelo has the decency to blush and I hear Carmela gasp while Miceli tries to stifle a laugh, but I feel his shoulders shake with mirth against mine. As the family continues to banter back and forth, I realize how much I'm enjoying it. They're very entertaining, mostly at each other's expense, but it's not mean-spirited. I have a feeling they would defend each other fiercely if the need arose.

Realizing that his family isn't going anywhere any time soon, Miceli asks Piero to set some more food out and then tells him we're all moving into the dining room for brunch together.

As we sit down, my heart flutters madly with the memory of what we did last night at this very table. I have a feeling Miceli is remembering as well because he sends me a very hot look then lowers his hand beneath the table cloth and lays it on my upper thigh. His fingers trace up and down, running along my inner thigh, and my breathing increases. Thank God, I didn't put my sundress on. Otherwise, I can't imagine where those naughty fingers of his would be right now.

Miceli sends me a wicked grin as he bites into a pastry, chewing slowly, dark eyes glued to me. I try not to notice how high his hand is roaming up my leg right now. How very close it's getting to my—

Ohhh. Sucking in a sharp breath, I reach for my orange juice and take a long sip. It doesn't do any good when it comes to cooling me off and I try to not react to the way he's slowly rubbing a finger up and down the seam of my leggings. Then he zeroes right in on my clit and presses firmly.

Electric tingles shoot through my lower body and my hand clenches so tightly around my glass, I'm scared it's going to shatter. Pressing my lips together, I realize someone just asked me a question and I can only blink.

"I'm sorry. What?" I ask as my lower body starts pulsing beneath Miceli's persistent and delicious touch.

14

MICELI

I wish Alessia was wearing her dress so I could slip my finger into her panties, but it seems like my touch is having the desired effect. I notice her hand shake, feel her thighs begin to tremble and I smirk, innocently chewing on my cherry danish.

Nothing gives me greater pleasure than making my wife come.

While she struggles to answer a question my brother just asked, I decide to show her sweet mercy and stop stroking. Deciding to finish what I started later, the moment my family is out that door, I give her thigh a final squeeze and bring my hand back up, grab my coffee and take a long, satisfying sip.

No matter how many times I fuck Alessia, I can't seem to get enough. Leaning back in my chair, I study her profile and wonder why that seems to be the case. I've always been able to have a good time with a woman, fuck her then walk away without a second thought. Actually, my second thought is I usually hope she doesn't become a clinger and start harassing me about a relationship. So, it still surprises the holy hell out of me that after knowing Alessia less than a day, I wanted to marry her.

Of course, she's beautiful, but I've bedded my fair share of women who were just as gorgeous. She's smart and sweet which I really like, too. And, that sassy mouth of hers has given me some delightfully charming comebacks. I took her innocence which is a big deal, and I suppose the only other virgin I slept with was my first way back when I was seventeen. We were both virgins at the time and it was awkward, fast and sloppy. I've refined my skills over the years and even learned a thing or two from an older woman I dated for a few weeks. Then, believe it or not, she thanked me for my time, said she hoped I learned something and moved on.

Shaking my head, I think about all of the lovers I've had over the years and they never meant a thing to me. Other than the physical pleasure we shared in the moment, there was nothing else. At least, I felt nothing on my end past my orgasm.

But now something is different. Something that I can't quite explain has changed. Alessia throws her head back and laughs at something Angelo says. He's such a playboy, worse than the rest of us, and has left a string of broken hearts in his wake. He could care less, though, and I can't ever see the smooth-talking charmer fall in love.

Enzo is thirty, two years older than Angelo, and is the sophisticated businessman out of us all. He's damn intelligent when it comes to numbers, figures and the stock market. He can make money without even trying anymore and keeps all of our portfolios brimming with cash. It's hard for me to picture him married, though, because his heart has always belonged to the Almighty Dollar.

Maybe Vin will get married one day, but that would require him to start living again and open himself up emotionally. Some bitch broke his heart years ago and he hasn't been the same since. He might get laid every once in a while, but that's the only "L" word he uses.

Turning my attention to Lottie, I stop all thoughts about sex. My baby sister is a dreamer who believes in love and that's all I care to know.

Imagining her getting it on with some guy makes my skin crawl and if the man she falls for ends up treating her badly, I can guarantee his ass will disappear with zero trace.

Even though I wasn't in any hurry to introduce my family to Alessia, I'm enjoying their interactions and how much they seem to love her. *How can they not?* I think watching my lovely wife charm them all with a story. Everything about her is fucking delightful. From her amazing sea-colored eyes to her gorgeous smile to the way she pulls my dick so deeply into her tight body that I nearly black out before coming.

My princess. *All mine.*

As much as I love my loud, outgoing family, I'm ready for them to leave after two hours of non-stop questions and conversation. They can be exhausting and I know they've overwhelmed Alessia. Hell, I'm tired. Besides, they've eaten every last drop of food and drank through three pots of coffee. Poor Piero has been serving us a bottomless brunch for hours.

Once I put out the hint that it's time for them to leave, they all get up and reluctantly head for the exit. I kiss my mother's cheeks. "I assume you're staying at the hotel?" I ask and she nods. We own a boutique hotel in the heart of the city and my parents usually stay there when they're visiting.

"Christmas is going to be so wonderful this year with Alessia joining us. You are planning to come to Sicily like usual, right?" my mom asks and I nod. No matter how busy our lives get, we always visit my parents' home during the holidays and stay at the winery. "I'm looking forward to it. And maybe there will even be a bambino in the oven."

My mouth edges up. If I have any say in the matter, there will definitely be a baby sooner rather than later. The almost overpowering urge—no, need—to procreate with Alessia and create a child with her isn't something I've ever felt before with anyone. I can't explain it, but somehow this amazing wife of mine has bewitched me.

After we all hug, kiss and say goodbye, Piero begins clearing the table and I turn to Alessia. "Well? What do you think of my crazy family? If I knew they were coming, I could've better prepared you."

Alessia looks up at me and gives me a huge smile. "I love them!" she exclaims. "They're so much fun. And they're the complete opposite of my serious parents and stoic sister. If I could build my own family from scratch, I'd create one exactly like yours."

My heart swells at her words. I didn't expect her to love them so much and I'm really glad it went well. "C'mere." I pull her into my arms and kiss her thoroughly. It's still only mid-afternoon, but I'm on the verge of dragging Alessia to bed, when she steps back, looking up at me with the most sincere expression.

"You're so lucky to have them as your family," she whispers.

"They're your family now, too," I tell her, laying a hand along her face.

"Thank you for sharing them with me." Then she yawns and I remember that I barely let her get any sleep last night. Deciding to be a good husband, I pull her into my arms and kiss the top of her dark, fragrant head. "How about a nap?"

Piero appears and I tell him to take the rest of the day off. I would like to be alone with my wife and not worry about Piero possibly walking in on us because there are still quite a few rooms we still need to christen.

"A nap?" she echoes doubtfully.

"I promise, I'll let you sleep. For a little while, anyway," I add mischievously and she chuckles.

"You're absolutely insatiable," she declares.

"Yeah, with you, I am completely insatiable." There's no point denying it. This little brunette minx makes me come undone in the best possible way and I'm starting to think she has me wrapped around that tiny finger of hers.

In order to keep my word and not jump her, I decide to avoid the bedroom and, instead, I lead her down to the big back area of the apartment where the ceilings soar. There's a huge, very comfy leather couch and I pull her down on it, spooning her. I love the way she curls up against my body, so soft and warm. So utterly trusting. Reaching over, I tug a blanket off the back of the couch and cover us up. Then I snuggle down, getting as close as possible, and press my face into the soft strands of her hair. Breathing deeply, wrapping my arm around her body, I close my eyes and rest.

Cuddled up with Alessia, I forget about everything else. She has this magical way of becoming my whole world. Eventually, her breathing evens out and becomes slow and even. Once I know she's asleep, I allow myself to drift off, too.

I'm not sure how much time passes, but when I open my eyes next, the sun has set and the room is dark, lit only by the city lights outside the large floor to ceiling windows. Alessia sighs softly and I press a kiss to her head.

"Are you awake?" I ask softly.

"Mmhmm," she murmurs, turning in my arms and stretching. Then she sits up and looks down at me. "I think that was the best nap I ever had."

"Me, too." I grab her hand and place a kiss along her knuckles. So soft.

Alessia lifts her attention from me and gazes around the room. "Do you play?" she asks.

"What?" I'm not sure what she's talking about until she nods to the piano in the corner.

"The piano," she clarifies, sliding off the couch.

"Oh, ah, no." I sit up, run a hand through my messy hair and scratch my chest. "Do you?"

I'm not sure what I'm expecting, but it isn't Alessia sitting down on the bench and running her fingers over the keyboard. Then they begin tapping the keys and a beautiful, melodic tune fills the air. For a stunned moment, I can only listen, shocked by how well she plays.

"I took lessons for ten years," she tells me, looking up and smiling, continuing to play without even a glance down at the keys.

I slip off the couch, stand up and walk over. Entranced, I watch the way her small, delicate fingers glide across the black and white keys, touching just the right spots to create a song. And I'm really fucking impressed. It's more than that, though. My chest squeezes and a sense of pride makes it swell.

"You're so good," I tell her, laying a palm on the piano's flat, black surface, leaning in and watching. I'm mesmerized, unable to look away. "What song is this?"

"Chopin's Nocturne in E Flat Major (Op.9 No.2)," she says, then gives me a shy smile. "Although, I'm afraid your piano is a bit out of tune, so it doesn't sound as good as it should."

"It sounds brilliant," I tell her, leaning even closer as the song speeds up slightly. "You're brilliant."

"I'm hardly Chopin, but I still enjoy playing. When I get the chance…"

"It sounds a little sad…and haunted," I say, watching how effortlessly she plays. My eyes are glued to her slim, extremely talented hands, and I can't look away. She's creating magic and it's beautiful.

Feeling my intense stare, she looks up and stops playing. "What?" she murmurs, looking self-conscious.

"Please, don't stop." I must have the strangest expression on my face, but I don't care.

"Haven't you ever seen anyone play the piano before?" she teases.

"Not like you." I nod at her. "Keep playing. Please."

"Okay." Her fingers start moving again and music fills the room.

That old saying about how music soothes the savage beast comes to mind. And, at this moment, it feels very true. I'm feeling so relaxed and absolutely engrossed in every stroke of her fingers against the keys. After several more minutes, she finishes the piece and looks up at me.

"I'm blown away."

"It's really not that big of a deal."

"It is. You're very talented, Alessia."

She scoots over and pats the bench. "I could always teach you."

But, I shake my head. "No, I'd rather sit here and listen to you play. I'm going to get the piano tuned for you. Or, would you like a new one? A bigger one?"

She laughs. "No. This one is lovely. It just needs a little TLC."

"Done. I'll have Piero call in the morning. But, on one condition." She lifts a delicate brow. "Will you play for me? Every night?"

"If you'd like."

Nodding, I cup her face and realize this woman is so much more beautiful than I even realized. And, it's her inside that's shining right now. So damn bright. Capturing her lips in a searing kiss, I drink deeply and feel my guard coming down. I think hers is lowering as well, and my heart twists in my chest as the truth pierces me like one of Cupid's arrows.

I am so utterly consumed with and smitten by my new wife that it's almost embarrassing. The more I get to know about her, the more besotted I become. I'm honestly not sure how I managed before her. Or, how she is becoming such a big part of my world in such a short amount of time. It's new and scary and so damn exhilarating.

Now that I've seen and tasted her sweet innocence, I can't imagine my life without her light in it.

15

ALESSIA

After another night spent in my new husband's arms, I'm not sore or tired. Miceli was almost a different man last night. He took his time and was so gentle. Each touch, each stroke, each kiss was almost, dare I say, done lovingly. He also made sure I got plenty of sleep and held me in his arms all night long.

I could definitely get used to it, too.

The next morning while eating a fluffy omelet prepared by Piero, I notice Miceli seems to be a little on edge. I'm learning to read him better and it's clear to me that something is bothering him.

"What's wrong?" I ask. "You're being extra quiet this morning."

He studies me for a long moment. "There's something I need to tell you."

My heart sinks. *Uh oh.* I lean forward and nod. "Okay, what?" I have no idea what to expect, but it isn't what he tells me.

"The other day at our meeting, Rocco Bianche wasn't happy, as I'm sure you can imagine." His deep breath is laced in sarcasm. Then he takes a deep breath and spills it, "Your father offered Gia's hand in place of yours."

"What?" Horror pours through me and a sick feeling settles in my gut. "Why would he do that?"

Miceli shakes his head. "Either he doesn't know about the rumors or he's unwilling to believe them."

No, Gia can't marry Rocco. Suddenly, the weight of the world settles on my shoulders and I know this is all my fault. If my sister is forced to marry that awful man and something bad happens, I will never be able to forgive myself.

"I need to talk to him. Maybe I can convince him to rescind his offer." My face screws up in a frown and I feel awful. I'm the one who was supposed to marry Rocco and now my poor sister is about to be tossed into the lion's den. "I can't let Gia get stuck with that monster. I can't! She's so broken, Miceli. This will push her right over the edge and I'll never be able to forgive myself."

"Calm down," he murmurs, standing up and walking around the table. His hands lay on my shoulders and he begins massaging the stressful knots away. As he continues rubbing and kneading, I tilt my head back and look up at him. "I think you might be able to sway him. I almost tried the other day, but I didn't want to press my luck."

"I have to try," I murmur. "I'd like to go over there today and talk to my father...and to Gia. She's going to act like it isn't a big deal in front of everyone, but once I get her alone, maybe she'll open up to me and we can figure out a way to stop this."

Miceli nods. "I have another meeting with the Five Families this afternoon, so you should probably go as soon as you can."

"Are you coming with me?" I ask, suddenly wanting him by my side.

He reaches for my hand, lifts it and presses a kiss to its back. I'm really growing to love when he does that and my heart kicks up a notch within my chest. It's such a sweet gesture from such a big, strong, extremely powerful man. "I have a meeting in less than an hour." His dark eyes search mine. "Would you like me to cancel it and come with you?"

"Oh, no. That's very thoughtful, but you go to your meeting and I'll try to persuade my father to see some sense."

"Are you sure?"

"I'm sure." I lift his hand to my lips and press a kiss to his knuckles this time. Heat swirls in the brown-black depths of his eyes and then he pulls me into his arms, kissing me hotly, deeply. My toes curl and I wrap my arms around his neck, my body melting against his firmness.

"I'm going to miss you," he whispers, dropping light kisses along my face.

Smiling, I pull back and press a hand to his chest. "You better leave before…" My voice trails off and we both know what I'm going to say. Before we end up in bed and cancel the entire day. Which is starting to sound better and better.

"Leaving," he murmurs, still pressing kisses against my cheekbone.

"Miceli!" I laugh softly and, after he kisses my lips one last time, he reluctantly steps back.

"I'll send Leo with you," he tells me.

"What about you? Who's going to watch over you?"

"I'll be fine," he assures me.

"You better be."

He runs his hands down the sides of my arms and grins. "Why? Would you miss me?"

"More than you know," I answer honestly. It's strange to think how much I've come to enjoy Miceli's company and how our worlds have seamlessly intertwined in such a short amount of time. The thought of him disappearing from my life forever makes my chest tighten.

"Sweet girl," he murmurs and kisses me one last time. "Go and see your family. And when we both get back home tonight, will you play the piano for me again?"

"Always. And I'll have dinner ready, too."

"You're making Piero's life much easier. I'll tell him he can leave at five if you don't need him for anything."

"That's fine. And I like cooking for us."

"And I love your cooking."

For a moment we both smile at each other and then he tells me Leo will be there momentarily. I watch Miceli walk out and think about how very different my life would be right now if Rocco Bianche were my husband. A shiver runs down my spine and I know that I need to do everything in my power to help Gia escape a future with that man.

Leo arrives shortly thereafter and drives me over to my family brownstone. It's strange not living here any longer, but I'm slowly growing accustomed to being in Miceli's large, bright home in the tallest skyscraper I've ever been in and on Billionaire's Row. It's strange to think how much money he has and I certainly don't think of his fortune as ours, despite being married to him.

After thanking Leo for driving me over, he gives me a funny look.

"I'm going in with you," he informs me. "As your bodyguard, my job is to keep you in my sight at all times."

"It's really not necessary," I tell him. "I'll be perfectly safe inside."

"Try telling that to Miceli." He gives me a dry look. "Stay put until I come around." Sliding out of the bullet-proof vehicle, Leo looks around the area, taking note of everyone and everything. He's very observant and I notice the way his hand lays over the gun hidden beneath his jacket. It's nice knowing he's here to watch over me when Miceli can't. Finally, after scoping out the situation, Leo walks around the SUV, opens my door and helps me out.

He guides me over to the stairs and we walk up together. I notice how he positions himself, keeping me covered in case anyone might try to shoot or attack.

"Were you in the military?" I ask. He moves like he's done this a thousand times before, so completely at ease with his role of protector.

"Special Forces," he tells me, but doesn't elaborate.

Hmm, well that explains a lot. I wonder how he and Miceli met. I'm about to ask when the door opens and my mother appears. I guess that conversation will be for another day.

My mom hugs me and we head into the living room where my father sits. Leo walks in with me, staying near the entrance, and my father's eyes flash with recognition.

"Leo," he states. "Glad to see you're watching over my daughter."

"Keeping Alessia safe is my number one priority, per Miceli."

My father nods and motions for me to come sit down. "I have a feeling I know what this is all about," he says, not looking too thrilled.

I don't even try to play it cool or pretend. Sweeping over, I sit down beside him and plead, "You can't make Gia marry Rocco, Dad. He's a monster and—"

"Monster?" my father echoes. "That's a bit dramatic, even for you Alessia."

"It's true," I insist, then look up to see Gia standing just outside the doorway. She glances over at Leo a moment too long then stands a little taller, facing off with us.

"I think I can speak for myself," she says coolly, her ice princess persona firmly in place. "But, thank you for your concern, Lessi."

I nod and press my lips together. If she needs me, I'll speak up, but she is right. My older sister can and will stand up for herself and let my father know exactly how she feels about the situation.

"Are you aware of the rumors?" she asks, sweeping into the room, right past Leo without a second look. I can't help but notice the way his eyes follow her, moving over her from head to toe. He's studying her so closely, so thoroughly, that I'd think he's accessing a threat. Then he must catch himself because he clears his throat and focuses on the view outside the window.

Very interesting, I think, watching them closely, gauging their quick interaction. *Leo and my sister?* They both come off as too serious and a little uptight at first, so I wonder how that would work? I have no idea if he's seeing anyone special, but I know poor Gia needs a good man who can help her move on from the wreckage of her last relationship. And I really like Leo. He's a great guy and that's exactly what my sister needs.

"Rumors don't equal truth, Gia," my father states.

"There's always a kernel of truth," I insist. "They don't just start from nothing."

My father sighs heavily. "Listen to me, girls. An alliance with the Bianche family would help us tremendously. Alessia was supposed to marry Rocco, but since that clearly didn't happen, Gia can. Why is this an issue? Don't tell me you believe the hearsay. Rocco's ex-fiancée left town after they had a fight. That's all."

I look over at my sister and Gia's caramel eyes narrow into slits. "First of all, Alessia and I are not just two women who can be interchanged and offered up to strange men."

The fierce and fiery tone in my older sister's voice has me stifling a grin. She is about to let loose on our father and I want to shout with glee, "Let him have it, sis!" Of course, I don't, but I do look over and see Leo's lips twitch. Apparently, he's just as amused as I am.

136

"We're living, breathing, feeling human beings who happen to be of the female persuasion, but that doesn't mean we can be given away like property. Because, if you haven't noticed, I am no one's chattel. I belong to me and this whole stupid thing of alliances and promises has lit a fire under my ass and woken me up."

I glance from Gia's red face to my mother who looks completely shocked, but happy, to Leo who's grinning widely now to my father who has a relatively calm expression on his face considering my sister is basically chewing him out.

But, Gia isn't finished and she continues, "When and if I decide to get married—and that's a very big if—I will choose who I decide to spend the rest of my life with. And, I'm sorry, Dad, but there's nothing you can do or say to convince me to marry Rocco Bianche. I almost made the mistake of giving in and going along with your wishes out of complacency, not duty. But, then I realized what a big mistake that would be. I am officially done with trying to please everyone else. From this point forward, the only one who I care about making happy around here is me!"

With a huff, Gia spins around on her heel, storms past Leo who now holds a hand over his mouth, and walks right out of the room.

"Well," my mother says, "I suppose it's good that Gia is, erm, feeling again. I was beginning to worry about her."

My dad sighs heavily. "Can you talk to her, Alessia? Smooth things over for me?"

"I'm not advising her to marry Rocco," I inform my father and stand up.

"I assumed you wouldn't."

With a nod, I head out and Leo follows on my heels.

"Well, that was entertaining," he murmurs.

"I haven't seen my sister that fired up since…" My voice trails off and I think about Marco and how happy she used to be. "Well, suffice it to say, it's been a while."

"She's been hurt."

It's not a question and I glance over at Leo. "Yes." I don't offer any further information and he doesn't ask. Once I reach Gia's closed bedroom door, I pause and look up at Leo. "Can you give us a minute alone?"

"I'll be right outside this door if you need me."

"Thank you." After a quick knock, I open the door, step inside and see Gia curled up in a chair, gazing out the window.

"I didn't say come in," she murmurs quietly, but without censure.

"I know." I close the door behind me and walk over, sitting down on the edge of her bed. "But, I had to tell you how glad I am that you stood up to father."

Gia finally looks over, her gaze moving beyond me as though searching for someone. *Leo maybe?* I wonder.

"He had it coming."

"He certainly did."

"If you're here to persuade me to change my mind—"

I shake my head. "Of course not. I'm on your side, Gia. Neither of us should be strong-armed into a marriage we don't want."

"It's a little too late for you," she comments, studying me closely, "but I have a feeling you're warming up quite nicely to your new husband."

My face flushes and I nod. "I am. But this isn't about me."

"I tried, you know," she says, voice soft, almost far away-sounding. "After Miceli stole you away, Rocco and I met." She hesitates.

"What happened?"

"He wasn't very nice and seemed to enjoy talking down to me. He even said I was his second choice and he didn't appreciate getting stuck with Miceli's leftovers."

"What an ass," I fume.

"He isn't happy and even claimed you were still his. He's very angry that Miceli swooped in and stole his 'future wife.' To the point where he was saying crazy things that started to scare me. He really thinks he has some sort of claim over you, Lessi." Her gaze wanders over to the door where Leo stands just on the other side of it. "I'm glad Miceli has someone with you when he can't be."

Her ominous words make my gut curdle. "Well, Rocco has no claim over me or you. And if he comes near me, I have Miceli or Leo to help. They're always nearby."

"Good. Just be careful. Rocco talks like you belong to him."

"We belong to ourselves."

"What about Miceli?" she asks, eyeing me closely.

"He doesn't own me, but if I had to belong to someone, I don't think I'd mind him as my keeper."

"He treats you well?"

"Like a princess," I tell her and smile.

And he truly does. In every possible way.

16

MICELI

It seems like every time I have to leave, it gets harder and harder because all I want to do is spend time with Alessia. The more I get to know about my wife, the more time I want to spend with her...

What is happening with me? I wonder.

Swallowing back the surge of feelings threatening to overflow and the very real truth that I'm falling for her, I return my full attention to the meeting at hand. As usual, everyone is arguing and I'm getting damn tired of it. Keeping peace among the Five Families is almost an impossible feat and I feel like I'm the sucker who's been charged with the monumental and very annoying task.

"Stop," I say without much force. Of course, Rocco keeps bitching at Caparelli and I grind my back molars. "Enough!" I yell and everyone finally shuts up.

"For God's sake, can't we have a rational conversation without it escalating to World War 3?" Milano asks.

"Apparently not," I answer, my voice dry as I level my unblinking stare on Rocco. He's always the one instigating these fights and he's really starting to piss me off. To the point where I'm not going to be able to hold back much longer. The asshole is going to get a beatdown from my fists.

"Things need to change," Rocco insists. "I'm tired of living according to what our great grandfathers decided way too many years ago."

"What're you saying?" I ask, my eyes narrowing in annoyance and disapproval. Christ, all I want to do is pound this asshole into the ground. "We throw out the truce? Enter into a full-on turf war with each other?"

"That's not smart for business," DeLuca comments.

"No, it's not," I instantly agree.

Rocco glares at me. "All I'm saying is times have changed. This isn't nineteen-fucking-twenty any longer. So, either get with the program or get out of the way."

This all boils down to the East side and how Rocco and the Bianche family want control over the illegal businesses there. But, Milano handles all aspects of that neighborhood.

Trying to ignore the headache pounding to life, I get up, shoving my chair back, and stalk over to the large, yellowed map hanging on the wall. One that was pinned up there so long ago by our ancestors, the edges are frayed and it's torn in several places.

"In case you've forgotten, Bianche, this is your area of the city." I stab my finger on the Northwest corner of town. "If you try to take over outside of your designated area, we're going to have a big fucking problem. You hear me?"

Rocco must be feeling ballsy today because he also shoves up out of his seat and stomps over to the map.

"That's no longer enough area for my family," he argues. "We want to expand and we can handle the narcotics side much better than the Milano's. They're doing a shit job."

"Fuck you," Milano snaps.

"Not an option," I say simply without giving a reason and this seems to infuriate Rocco all the more.

"Who the fuck do you think you are, Rossi? Why do you get to call all the shots?"

Suppressing a sigh, I look over at the men sitting at the round table. And the very reason it's round is because there is no head man in charge. No one is sitting at the head of the table because there purposely isn't one. We're all supposed to be equals with a fair share in this city.

"This is a democracy," I say, striving to remain calm. But, damn, Rocco is testing me. Stretching my patience to the absolute limits. "If you want something to change then we need to vote."

Rocco rolls his eyes and crosses his arms because he knows he has already lost. No one wants to give up one block of their territory.

"Milano, do you have anything else to add?" I ask, looking directly at Dominic Milano whose family is in charge of that section of town.

"We can handle it like we always have," he states firmly.

I nod then lay the vote on the table, anyway. Just to further incite a potential riot with Rocco. I'm hoping this will be a clean sweep and shut him up. Or, make his head explode in fury. *I'd like to see that actually,* I think with an inward chuckle. "All in favor of extending any of the Eastern neighborhoods to the Bianche family?"

No one raises their hand or voices a yay. Instead, a chorus of nay's fill the air. With a smug smirk, I cross my arms and level a look at Bianche.

"There you have it. Your family's control will remain right where it is."

"It's not enough!" he roars. "We're being cheated and it's only fair to give us more. You all know it!"

"Why don't you have a seat?" Aldo DeLuca says, trying to deescalate the situation.

"Yeah, Bianche, take a fucking seat." I probably should've kept my mouth shut, but I can't. Images of Alessia fill my head and it makes me physically ill to think this snake almost got ahold of her. My sweet, innocent, sassy woman.

"You think I take orders from you?" Rocco turns and spits on the floor. "Think again, *stronzo.*"

Gritting my teeth, I lower my hands and clench my fists. This is not going to end well. I already know it.

"You're a fucking thief, Rossi," Rocco continues, "and you just keep stealing from us all."

My blood pressure skyrockets, nostrils flaring, at what he's inferring. "I haven't stolen anything," I growl.

"You think you're in charge and can call all the shots and keep the best territory for your family. You think we all haven't noticed?"

"I didn't take anything. It's not my fault that my family ended up with the neighborhoods we did. But, it is my fault that I've managed to make all of their businesses prosper and grow into so much more than they ever were. Because unlike you, I work hard and don't just run around like a little weasel looking for handouts and to prosper off other people's hard work."

"You take what doesn't belong to you. What *never* belonged to you," he insists.

Of course, I see exactly where this is going. He's talking about Alessia and how he lost her. Well, you know what? Too fucking bad. "You got something to say?" I take a threatening step closer.

"Alessia was mine and you stole her! You kidnapped her and forced her to marry you. That woman was promised to me!"

"You sound like such a whiny, little bitch. Alessia is mine. She was never yours."

"Yes, she was!"

Before I can say another word, Rocco launches himself into me. We both go flying backwards and hit the floor with an oomph. Wrestling around, I manage to get a few good hits in, but I also take a few, too. The man is completely unhinged which seems to be making him utterly reckless and much stronger than he usually is.

"Stop! Break it up, you two!"

But, we ignore Caparelli and the others and keep throwing punches. Rocco's knuckles make contact with my temple really fucking hard and his ring cuts deep, slicing the skin there. Jerking back, blood drips down the side of my head as I knee him in the side so hard he yells an obscenity.

Two sets of arms grab me and pull me back. At the same time, someone grabs Rocco, too, forcing us to break up our little fight. Breathing hard, blood oozing from my head and sliding into my eye, I yank free of the older men holding me and give my suit jacket a shake.

"How fucking dare you lay hands on me," I say, my voice low. A deadly whisper.

Panting and completely winded, Rocco pulls against Milano who is still restraining him. He looks feral with a wild, almost demented look in his dark eyes. "You shouldn't be in charge. You're going to destroy everything."

Struggling not to roll my eyes, I chalk his whiny words up to jealousy. He's pissed because I have Alessia and my businesses are all doing better than his. As they well should be since I work my ass off while he likes to hit the whore houses and party it up nearly every night.

"You should just go back to Sicily," he continues. "Go pick grapes at your parents' vineyard."

"Do you think I give a rat's ass what a piece of shit like you thinks?" I ask calmly.

"Miceli..." I feel Caparelli place a hand on my shoulder.

After straightening my tie, I swipe the blood away that's stinging my eye and whip it onto the floor. "You listen to me, Bianche—stay away from Alessia and her sister."

"Maybe Alessia wants me," he goads, shrugging off Milano's grip. "Did it ever occur to you that she never chose you? That she'd much rather have my dick sliding into her wet cunt every night?"

A fury like I've never felt before erupts within me and a red haze settles over my vision right before I pull the gun I'm not supposed to bring into this room. Ever. At nearly the same time, every single man, including Rocco, also pulls a pistol.

So much for following the rules of no weapons allowed in the meeting room.

We each aim our guns at each other and it's like a damn Mexican standoff. Steady fingers hover on triggers and faces are grim. No one appears willing to back down, either. I have no idea how this is going to end. I guess probably not well.

"I'm glad to see we've all ignored the no weapons rule," Caparelli comments dryly.

"Fuck off," Milano says. "We all know you've been bringing a gun into these meetings for the past year."

As the tension escalates, I know I need to put a stop to this before everyone starts shooting and we all kill each other.

"Gentlemen, I'm sorry for dragging you into a personal issue." My voice resonates with calm, steely confidence. "I suggest we all put our weapons away and resume conversations later after we've all had time to cool off."

"Agreed," DeLuca says, backing me up.

Very slowly, I lower my gun and tuck it back under my jacket, returning it in my waistband. We're going to need to put up metal detectors to keep this shit from happening again because right now…

Right now, no one trusts anyone. And that's a precarious spot to be in with a group of people fighting to control the city.

Rocco is the last man to lower his pistol and he glares at me as he does so. "You think you won, don't you?" he asks. Before I can respond, he continues, "You haven't won shit, Rossi. In fact, if I have anything to say about it, you're going to lose everything."

"Really?" I drawl, refusing to let him rile me up again, smoothing my hands down the front of my suit. I refuse to show an ounce of fear or even concern at his idle threats. Because that's all they are and I don't take him seriously. He just likes to puff his chest out and play big man on campus. But, the truth is Rocco Bianche will never amount to anything more than a woman-killing, whoring, lazy piece of shit.

I'm tempted to tell him exactly what I'm thinking when he dares to take a step closer. Pointing a finger at me, he hisses, "Mark my words, you're going to regret what you did. Because I'm going to make sure you pay."

I roll my eyes. "Fuck off, Bianche," I tell him, keeping my voice level and bored-sounding. I'm tired of dealing with this clown and he needs to be taught a lesson about respect if he thinks he's still going to sit at this table with the other families. Because right now, I'm planning to do everything in my power to see that he's permanently removed.

There are other far more competent people in his family who can step up and take over.

He nods slowly, a twisted smile cracking his face. "You'll see." Then he storms out, his bodyguard following on his heels.

Once Bianche is gone, my shoulders slump slightly and the tension I've been holding onto releases a bit.

"You better watch your back, Rossi," Caparelli advises and the others nod.

"You think I'm scared of that sack of shit?" My face screws up and I make a scoffing sound.

"No…but maybe you should be."

"Don't take his threat lightly," Milano states. "He's gone off the deep end and is out for blood."

"Your blood," Caparelli comments.

Because I took Alessia, I think, but I don't say another word. That must be the reason, but this meeting is over and I'm done talking. With a sharp nod, I walk out.

17

ALESSIA

The moment I hear the elevator door ding, I know Miceli is home and my heart soars. It's strange how easily I slipped into domestic bliss. But, here I am, bending over and pulling out a batch of freshly-made manicotti from the oven.

The low rumble of masculine voices echoes into the kitchen and Miceli and Leo must be talking. Leo was hanging out in the kitchen with me for a while and I couldn't help but smile when he nonchalantly navigated our conversation to Gia. He seemed very interested in my sister after seeing her earlier today, but he tried to play off very casually. Typical man. I'm very observant, though, and I'm pretty sure he's interested in getting to know her better. I'll have to mention him to Gia next time we talk and see how she reacts.

I carry the hot tray into the dining room and set it down on an oven mitt. The rest of the table is set and just as I lift the serving spoon, Miceli and Leo appear. My mouth drops open when I see the dried blood on Miceli's face.

"Oh, my God, what happened?" I rush over to get a closer look ."Are you okay?"

Miceli leans down and kisses me, his lips so gentle and soft. Then he pulls back and tucks a loose strand of hair behind my ear. "I'm fine. But we have some things to discuss. I invited Leo to join us, so I hope there's enough?"

"Oh, there's plenty." I frown, eyeing the dried blood caked on his temple. "Are you sure you're okay?"

Miceli nods. "Let me wash up and I'll be right back." His attention moves over to the table and he sniffs the air. "It smells divine."

"I made manicotti. Do you need any help?"

"No, but thank you." He drops another kiss on my lips and then walks away. I look over at Leo and wring my hands, clearly upset. "Is he really okay?" I ask.

"He'll be fine."

Pulling my lower lip into my mouth, I decide we all need a glass of wine to settle our nerves. Mine especially. "Have a seat," I tell Leo. "I'm going to get some wine."

"Good idea."

After I grab a bottle and some glasses, I return to the dining room and Miceli is already back. He takes the bottle from me and twists the cork out. While he pours us each a glass, I dish out the food.

"Okay, spill it," I say after we both sit down. "What happened to your head?"

"Rocco and I got into a fight. Some punches were thrown, but I'm fine."

I hope he's telling me the truth and not trying to be macho and hide his pain. "Are you sure? You don't need stitches?"

"No, but thank you for the concern."

"He's been hit a lot harder than by Rocco's pissy-ass fists," Leo interjects.

"You weren't even there," I say. "That cut could be from falling down and hitting his head. He could have a concussion. Are you sure you're okay?"

Miceli reaches for my hand and squeezes. "Yes, princess. Promise."

My nerves relax slightly and I nod. But if he thinks I'm not going to take a closer look later and make him take some aspirin then he's got another thing coming. The mama bear in me has woken up and I will make sure my man is taken care of. "What happened?"

Miceli fills both of us in about what went down during the meeting and my stomach clenches with dread. Dropping my fork, my appetite disappears, and I reach for my wine glass. After I take a sip, I frown. This conversation is making me sick to my stomach. The idea that Rocco threatened Miceli concerns me on a very deep level. If anything happens to Miceli, there will be hell to pay. I'll make sure of it.

"Then he just stormed out?" Leo asks, stuffing a forkful of manicotti into his mouth.

Miceli nods, biting into a hunk of buttered bread. "Of course, he went out spewing bullshit about making me pay and puffing his chest out. Typical Rocco."

"Making you pay?" I echo.

"Don't worry. He's an idiot and there's no reason to be scared of him, okay? He's all talk. He always has been."

Even though he's trying to reassure me, I still feel uncertain and fear- ful. I don't like the idea of someone threatening my husband. Leo just scoffs and is so busy shoving food in his face that he doesn't seem overly concerned. Maybe if they're both relaxed then I should be, too.

But, even though I tell myself that, I'm still anxious. A part of me also wonders if Miceli is leaving something out. I get a feeling he might be in order to protect and not worry me. Well, if that's the case, I'll make sure to pry it out of him later. I don't like secrets and I want to make sure I know exactly what's going on.

I manage to eat some more while they discuss what should be done about Rocco. In the end, Leo suggests Miceli lay low and not antagonize him further.

"But, it's so much fun," Miceli draws out, then sips his wine.

"Listen to your friend," I advise. "Now, who's ready for dessert?"

"Me!" Leo practically shouts.

I chuckle. "I'm going to go out on a limb and say you enjoy my cooking?"

"Best I ever had."

"You'd think you don't have food at your own house," Miceli says.

"I don't. Haven't been to the grocery store in weeks."

"Maybe it's about time you find a woman of your own," Miceli murmurs.

"Not quite ready for that."

"If you don't go grocery shopping then what do you eat?" I ask.

"Carryout mostly. So, feel free to invite me to stay for dinner any time," he adds with a mischievous grin.

"Duly noted," I say with a small smile then stand up and head into the kitchen to grab the fresh cannoli I picked up from the bakery earlier. We spend the next half an hour lingering over dessert and then I can tell Miceli is ready for Leo to leave. But, instead of dropping a subtle hint, he pushes his plate away and says, "Okay, you ate. Now get out."

Leo chuckles. "Okay, okay. I certainly don't want to wear out my welcome. Alessia, thank you for a wonderful dinner." His gaze turns to Miceli and grows serious. "Miceli, lay low, okay? If you need something, I can do it. Or, Piero. There's no sense in stirring more shit up right now or making yourself a target."

Miceli nods, but doesn't comment further on the subject. "See you tomorrow."

"You two have a good night." He tosses us a mischievous wink. "Don't stay up too late. Oh, and don't worry, I'll see myself out."

"Get outta here!" Miceli throws his napkin at Leo who disappears through the doorway with a laugh.

"I swear, if he wasn't my best friend..."

"You two are like brothers," I say. Standing up, I start to clear the table.

"Piero can clear the table. I want to hear my wife play the piano." Before I can respond, he grabs my hand and pulls me into the back room. A smile curves my mouth and I can't help but do as he asks. I love seeing the look that comes over his face as I play.

After I play a few Chopin nocturnes, Miceli pulls me onto his lap and things turn steamy fast. No matter how many times we're together, it never seems to be enough. Miceli shifts me around and when I'm straddling him, he leans into me, kissing me deeply, all tongue and heat. So much heat. My back hits the piano and several discordant notes fill the air as we continue to devour each other.

His hands are all over me and I sigh into his mouth, loving the way he kisses and touches me. When he suddenly pulls back, I frown. "What's wrong?"

"I think Leo is right. We should both lay low for a while because Rocco and his allies can't be trusted. I don't want you leaving this house. Okay? Can you promise me that?"

His concern makes my heart swell, but I am just as worried about him. However, I know there's no way he's going to stay home like he should. He always has a meeting. "And do you promise to take Leo with you everywhere you go?"

"I promise."

"Then I should probably tell you that I have a doctor's appointment tomorrow."

"Why? What's wrong?" His face screws up in worry.

"Nothing. It's just a checkup." I'm not being completely upfront with him and the truth is I have a nagging suspicion that I might be pregnant. But, the last thing I want to do is say that. Miceli is under a lot of stress with the other families, especially after what happened today. I don't want to add to his plate and there's a very good possibility that I'm not pregnant. So, instead of obsessing over it like I've been doing, I decided to just make an appointment and find out one way or another. We've been having unprotected sex from the beginning and it's been just over a month now. For all I know, it might even still be too early for the doctor to tell. I really have no idea since I've never been pregnant before.

"I'm going with you," Miceli announces.

"Are you sure? I can take Leo—"

"No. I'll be right there with you," he insists, and I smile.

God, this man is doing things to me that make my head spin and my body sing. Our mouths collide and I bump into the piano keys again sending another random few notes into the air. From there, our night gets much more steamy and Miceli sends me spiraling off into one amazing orgasm after another.

I seriously wonder how I ever got so lucky. Because I truly feel like the most blessed woman in the world.

The next day, Miceli accompanies me to the doctor's office, and he even has Leo drive us over. I feel like I'm part of a hot man entourage and have never felt safer in my life, dwarfed between my two very tall, very muscled guardians. No one in his right mind would try something with these two hovering around. They look like they could take on the entire world, much less easily stop one bad guy.

While Leo waits for us outside, giving us some privacy, Miceli is my shadow. I tell him he doesn't have to go into the exam room with me, but he's insistent. Even though he's seen, touched and licked every crevice of my body, I'm not sure how I feel about him going in with me. Not like I can change his mind, though, because once Miceli decides he's doing something, there's no way to dissuade him.

While we're sitting in the waiting room, his phone rings. Miceli excuses himself and steps into the hall. He reappears almost instantly and his normally tanned face looks white.

"What's wrong?" I ask, standing up and moving over to meet him.

"Enzo was shot. He was just rushed to the hospital and...it's not looking good."

"Oh, my God."

The nurse appears and calls my name, motioning for me to follow her. "The doctor is ready for you, Mrs. Rossi."

Miceli looks beyond shocked and I touch his arm. "Let me reschedule my appointment. I'll come to the hospital with you."

"Mrs. Rossi?" the nurse calls again.

But, he shakes his head. "No. Go see the doctor. You're already here and they're ready for you. I'll have Leo come in here and wait for you. After you're finished, I want him to drive you straight home. I'll call you with an update."

"Okay." Even though I'd rather go with him, I'm not going to stand here and waste time arguing. If his brother is barely hanging onto life, Miceli needs to get to the hospital as soon as possible. Before he can leave, I push up onto my toes and press a reassuring kiss to his lips. "It'll be okay."

"I'll see you soon."

I watch as Miceli walks away, my heart heavy. I hope my words are true and that everything will be alright. Worry consumes me, but I follow the nurse to the exam room and go through with the appointment by myself. Even though I didn't originally want Miceli in the examination room with me, I find myself missing his presence and wishing he was in here after all.

And, I discover that I am right. The doctor tells me I'm almost five weeks pregnant which means I must've conceived on the night we were married. My nerves flutter and it's a strange, scary kind of excitement. How is Miceli going to react? I honestly have no idea. Is this too soon? I'm thinking he must want a baby because he's taken me bare from the very first time we had sex.

I'll have to come up with the perfect way to tell him, especially now with Enzo being shot. God. What the hell happened? Who shot him? My mind is a flurry of questions and anxiety.

After quickly getting dressed, I hurry out to the waiting room and see Leo standing near the exit, waiting for me. He pushes off the wall, straightening up, when he sees me. "Are you ready?"

"Yes, let's go. Have you heard anything else about Enzo?"

Leo shakes his head. "Not yet. Miceli said to take you straight home. He's going to call with an update."

I nod. "I can't believe this. Poor Enzo."

Leo leads me down the hall and carefully opens the front door. We step outside and as we walk around the corner, heading to the small lot where the car is parked, a large SUV with dark-tinted windows screeches up. The doors fly open and two men jump out, guns in hand.

Everything happens so fast. Leo yells for me to get down, shoving me behind him and blocking me with his large body as gunshots crack through the air. The ominous POP POP POP has me dropping, my knees scraping the pavement and my hands covering my head. Voices fill the air and when someone falls to the pavement, I lift my head and see Leo lying there, eyes wide and coughing up blood.

"Leo!" I screech and scramble over. Blood is everywhere, splattered across the pavement, and horror and panic for Leo propel me straight over to him. But, before I can reach him, two strong hands grab me and lift me up off the ground.

"Let me go!" I yell. "Help! Somebody help m—"

A large, beefy hand slaps over my mouth, stifling my cries for help, and then I'm dragged backwards and tossed into the waiting SUV. The car takes off and I slam against the back of the seat. I can't believe this is happening and I have no idea where we're going. Or, what's going to happen.

Right at that moment, Miceli's words come back to haunt me, reverberating through my head: *"I don't think that man was trying to kill me. I think he was after you."*

I didn't believe it at the time, but now? Now I'm not so sure.

18

MICELI

On my way to the hospital, I call my brother Vin and ask what the hell is going on.

"What're you talking about?" he asks, sounding confused. Calm, too. He sounds damn calm considering our brother is near death.

"Enzo was shot! I'm on my way to the hospital and—"

"Enzo is sitting right here next to me," Vin interrupts. "Who the hell told you he was shot?"

"Shot?" I hear Enzo's voice clear as day.

Lifting my foot up off the gas pedal, slowing down, I frown. "An enforcer called and told me. Shit." The hissed curse escapes my mouth and I think I've been played.

"Don't go to the hospital," Vin warns.

"Yeah," I say slowly, braking and pulling over to the curb. "Fuck. Do you think it's some kind of setup?"

"Could be. I can send some men over to check it out. Meanwhile, stay far away from that hospital. Something is definitely off."

I know my brother is right and suddenly I'm paranoid, glancing in the rear view mirror. I start driving again, turning down side streets, and trying to determine if anyone is following me.

As if he can see what I'm doing, Vin asks, "Do you notice anyone suspicious on your tail?"

"No. It doesn't look like anyone is following me." My call waiting beeps and I look down to see Leo's name flashing. "That's Leo, I need to take it. Call you back." I disconnect the call with my brother and answer Leo. "Leo, what's up?"

"Your friend Leo's been shot," a strange voice says. "He asked me to call you right before he passed out."

"What?" My heart starts thumping madly and shock hits me like a punch in the gut. What the fuck is going on? Now Leo's shot? I don't know what to believe. In the background, I can hear ambulance sirens screaming. "Who is this?"

"Just a guy who stumbled onto the scene. I called 911 and they're coming now. But your friend was insistent that I call you. He doesn't look good, man. I don't know—"

"What about the woman with him?" I force out between clenched teeth, already dreading the answer that I know is coming.

"What? There's no woman with him."

My entire world seems to tip and a sickening terror fills me. Where is Alessia? I try to tell myself to think logically. Maybe she ran off to get help or she might still even be inside the doctor's office. But I know neither one of those things is true.

Someone distracted me then took full advantage of my absence. They took Leo down and now Alessia is missing.

"You don't see a woman anywhere?" I ask again.

"No. I just saw this guy on the ground. He's bleeding a lot."

Fuck. Everything inside me panics for just a brief moment before I reel it back in and force myself to retake control.

"Text me what hospital they're taking my friend to...please." *Hang in there, Leo.*

"Sure thing," the guy responds and I can hear the paramedics arriving. "They're here."

"Thank you." I hang up, pull over to the curb and take several deep breaths, telling myself to calm down. I can't lose my shit right now, but I am precariously close. My wife has disappeared into thin air and my best friend is bleeding out on the pavement.

After several deep breaths, I call Vincentius back up. "Vin, Leo is the one who was shot and the ambulance is taking him to—" My phone beeps with a text and I see the answer I need. "—St. Vincent's Hospital. Can you go there right now? He was with Alessia..."

My voice cracks and a tidal wave of emotion powers through me.

"Where's Alessia?" Vin asks.

"I don't know," I force out and swipe a hand through my hair.

"Don't lose your shit, Miceli. Enzo and I will meet you at the hospital. I'll call Angelo, too. Keep it together, bro. We're going to find her, okay?"

I don't say anything. Just swallow back the bile rising in the back of my throat.

"Okay?" he repeats again, and I give my head a hard shake.

"Yeah, okay. See you there." After disconnecting the call, I hit the gas and pull away from the curb. If we can't talk to Leo, I'm not sure how we're going to know what happened and how the hell we're going to be able to find Alessia. But I have to believe it. If anyone can find her, the four of us can.

And, God willing, we will.

By the time I reach the hospital, I know I was set up and I am livid. Storming through the front doors, I glance around and spot Angelo who waves to me and hurries over. My youngest brother is a carefree flirt, but the usual smile on his face is absent.

"Miceli! This way."

Our long strides take us to the elevator quickly and we step inside.

"How's Leo?" I ask, unable to keep the worry out of my voice.

"He's in surgery right now," Angelo informs me. "He's not in good shape. Took three bullets to the chest."

"Fuck." I squeeze my eyes shut and swear the worst kind of vengeance on whatever motherfuckers took my best friend down. *Down, but not out,* I remind myself. "He has to make it."

Angelo nods. "He's a tough SOB. The doctor said he'll keep us updated."

When the door opens again, we step out and Angelo leads me down to the waiting area near the operating room where Leo is currently being saved. I see Vin and Enzo who are sitting in chairs, waiting. They jump up as we walk over and I grab Enzo in a half-hug and slap his back.

"They told me you're the one who'd been shot." Relief that my brother is okay fills me, but I'm terrified for Leo and Alessia. "Any news?"

"Nothing yet," Vin states. "Any word on Alessia?"

I scrub a hand down my face. "Nothing. And I'm starting to freak the fuck out."

For a moment, no one says anything. There's nothing to say. How can we make a plan to get my wife back when I have no idea who took her or where she is? Is someone going to demand a ransom? Is this the same asshole who sent the gunman after her outside of Penn Station? Is she still even alive?

That last thought makes my knees give out and I drop down in a chair and slide my hands through my hair, pulling hard. I've never felt so goddamn helpless in all of my life and it's killing me. Alessia needs me now more than ever and there's nothing that I can do.

Or, is there?

I lift my head up, a plan coming together. "I rule this city and have eyes and ears everywhere." My brothers focus on me and nod. "So, why not put out a 911 bulletin to all of my enforcers and informers? To every single contact I have in the underworld? And that you all have, too?"

"I can do that," Enzo immediately says. "I have contacts everywhere in the business world. Someone might've heard something."

"We can all put feelers out," Angelo says and Vin nods in agreement.

If I'm being honest, though, my gut is leaning heavily toward Rocco Bianche. "I have no proof, but I want to check out Rocco Bianche. I don't trust the snake and he thinks he might still have some sort of claim on Alessia."

"On it," Vin states, pulling his phone from his pocket.

"And I'll set some calls in motion," Enzo tells me, also starting to dial someone.

"I'll see if I can get an update on Leo," Angelo offers and walks away at a brisk pace.

I feel better knowing my brothers are on it and their support steadies me. It means the fucking world. I'm not sure what I would do without them. Usually, as the oldest, I'm the pillar and the one offering his support to everyone else, but they're stepping up just like I need them to do at this moment and I know I can count on them.

In the meantime, I decide to make some calls of my own. I put the word out that my wife is missing and anyone with information will be obscenely rewarded, both financially and by me personally. Me saying that I will owe someone a favor is a really big fucking deal. And anyone who helps me find Alessia will be eternally in my good graces. I will quite literally owe them everything because the indisputable truth is I am head over heels in love with my wife.

Nothing bad is going to happen to her, I tell myself, repeating the mantra over and over again. I refuse to accept the possibility that things could turn out differently. I need her back in my arms and my best friend out of surgery. As if on cue, Angelo reappears.

"Leo made it," he assures me and I prop a hand against the wall as relief fills me. "It was touch and go there for a minute. He lost a lot of blood, but the doc extracted two bullets and the third one passed through his shoulder."

"Jesus," I hiss.

"The doc doesn't know when he'll be awake, so we won't be able to talk to Leo about what happened for a while yet."

My phone starts buzzing and I look down at the caller ID to see the name of an old informant of mine. A loner who lives in the shadows, but he's smart and well-connected. Although he's never divulged anything personal about himself, and I certainly don't ask questions, I get former military vibes from the guy. Probably some kind of ghost ops.

"Archer," I say in greeting, using his last name. Hell, I don't even know his first name.

"Rossi," he returns evenly in a deep, slightly gravelly voice. "I have some intel that you might want."

"Go ahead."

"Bianche's house is lit up like a Christmas tree and I've been told—from an extremely reliable inside source—that he has your new wife."

I let out a vicious curse and damn Rocco Bianche's soul to eternal hell. I fucking knew it. Fighting back the urge to start throwing things, I pull in a deep breath. "Can you get me a floor plan of Bianche's mansion?"

"Already got it."

My phone vibrates with an email and I let out a relieved breath. "Thank you, Archer. I owe you."

He lets out a half-snort. "Trust me, Rossi. You don't want to owe me shit."

The call disconnects and I look at Angelo. "Bianche has her."

"Who was that?"

"A trusted source. Guy's a ghost, though, so I don't know much about him personally. But he has the inside connections necessary to get information. He just sent me the floor plans to Bianche's house."

Right on time, I see Vin and Enzo striding toward us and I quickly fill them in on the call from Archer.

"So, what's the plan?" Enzo asks, crossing his arms.

Even though I'm itching to go in with guns blazing, I know that we need to play this smart. I can't be careless and potentially put Alessia in harm's way. "We have to be fast and discreet," I tell them. "And we have to move now. Is everyone carrying?"

They all nod, and I can't express how grateful I am that they immediately have my back.

"Let's go," Vin says. "We'll take Miceli's SUV because it's bulletproof. And we'll come up with a plan on the way there."

There is no time to waste and I appreciate that they recognize this. We are going to bring Rocco down and I'm going to get Alessia back. Because I know now without a doubt that I can't live without her—she's the love of my life and I'll die to protect her. To save her.

I just hope and pray that we're not too late and Rocco hasn't done anything stupid. Because if he's touched one silky strand of hair on my wife's head, I'm going to empty my gun into him and send his black soul straight to hell where he belongs.

19

ALESSIA

I have no idea what is happening and I squeeze my eyes shut, sending out a mental plea. *Please, God, please let Leo be okay.* The image of him lying there on the ground, bleeding profusely, is burned into my brain. Even though it didn't look good, I hope that I'm wrong. If Leo dies, I don't know if I'd ever be able to forgive myself. He was guarding me and took every one of those bullets to protect me. Tears burn the back of my eyes, but I will them away, knowing that I need to be strong and focused right now.

First Enzo, then Leo...who's next?

Bouncing around on the backseat of the SUV, I don't know where we're going, much less who abducted me. But, I try to remain as calm as possible and not panic because that won't help anything.

Discovering I'm pregnant with our child has put me in a completely different mindset than I was in before. Because it's not just my life on the line right now. I also have my unborn baby to protect. And, I will fight like a tiger to make sure he or she remains safe.

Even though I have no idea who is responsible for kidnapping me, I do know that both Miceli and my father have a lot of common enemies. And now that I'm connected to two of the most powerful mafia families in the city—one by blood and one by marriage—it only makes sense that bad people might think they can use me as some kind of bargaining chip or leverage to get what they want.

But, I refuse to be someone else's pawn in this game of mafia kingpins. Especially now that an innocent baby is involved. No matter what happens, I will defend mine and Miceli's child until my very last breath. So, for the time being, I sit back and don't say a word. I need these men to believe I am not a threat and will cooperate. The last thing I want to do is draw attention to myself or make them believe I'm going to be trouble. I want to lull them into a false sense of security so they will inevitably underestimate me at just the right moment. And, hopefully, that will aid in my eventual escape.

We leave the city and drive for a while. I keep my attention fixed outside the dark-tinted window, trying to figure out where we could possibly be going. After what feels like forever, I see a huge estate set back from the road. The house is far larger than anyone would ever need and it's surrounded by tall trees. The entire estate is circled by an extremely high, wrought iron fence with sharp-looking points on top, and I watch the driver hit a remote. The front gate slowly swings inward and we pull forward, heading down the very long, gravel driveway.

Heart in my throat, my nails dig into the leather seat and I lean forward, trying to get a better look as we drive closer. The house is white with large pillars and it looks like there are four or five floors. There are so many windows, I can't even count them all and lights burn brightly inside. Yet, nothing about it feels welcoming. In fact, I feel like we're pulling up to the doorway to hell and every flickering light in the windows remind me of flames. Flames trying to reach out and burn me.

Shifting in my seat, I wait as the car comes to a complete stop. I could try to make a run for it, but I have a feeling that won't end well. These men are most likely just as fast as they are strong. Plus, they have guns and know the layout of the property which puts me at an immediate disadvantage. I'm in the dark and without a weapon. The better option, at this time, is for me to figure out what's going on and make an informed decision when the time comes. Because I will get out of here, one way or another.

The SUV's back door opens and the huge thug who dragged me into the car earlier motions for me to get out. "Let's go," he grumbles impatiently.

I slide out of the vehicle and look up at the intimidating house, rubbing the chill from my arms. And that's when I see the fancy letter written in cursive on a plaque above the front door. It's the letter "B."

As in "B" for Bianche.

My heart sinks with dread. Why would I be stolen away and brought out here to the Bianche estate? Would Rocco really be so bold? And why? *What's the point,* I wonder? *What in the world can he possibly want?*

An enforcer opens the door and the thugs escort me inside and down to an office where Rocco sits at his desk.

"Finally," he says, standing up and walking around the large desk. "That took much longer than I thought it would. I can't imagine she gave you any trouble."

"Not her, but that huge bodyguard with her didn't make the situation very easy. Took three bullets to bring him down."

"You killed Leo Amato, Miceli's number one man?" Rocco's voice is filled with disbelief, awe and something else…what almost sounds like hope.

Bastard.

"Hell yeah," the man responds, and Rocco gives him an oily smile.

"Remind me to give you a raise," Rocco says and I feel like I'm going to vomit. "You're sure no one followed you here?"

"Positive."

"Good."

Leo can't be dead. Guilt pours over me in waves and I make the mistake of dropping my hands and covering my belly. Which, of course, Rocco notices.

"Leave," he suddenly snaps. "Alessia and I have things to discuss in private."

Even though I know it's best to be accommodating and to play it safe, anger rears its ugly head and I'm so angry I could spit. How dare Rocco think he can just pluck me off the street and drag me here against my will. And, if he thinks he's still marrying my sister then he has another thing coming.

"Since when did you start kidnapping women, Rocco?" I ask, my voice dry as a high desert wind.

"It's hardly kidnapping when you belong to me, Alessia."

"Belong to..." My voice trails off in astonishment. "What're you talking about? I don't belong to anyone, but if I did, I belong to Miceli."

"No, you don't!" he roars angrily, face turning a mottled shade of reddish-purple, and I take a surprised step back. "You were always supposed to be mine. Everyone knew your father promised you to me and now I'm cashing in on that. He must honor his word."

"It's too late," I say, stating the obvious, searching his wild, black eyes. "I'm married to—"

"Don't say his name," he snaps. "From this point forward, you aren't to think about him or talk about him or ever refer to him again. As far as I'm concerned, Miceli Rossi is dead which means you are no longer his wife."

Rocco is talking like a crazy person and I'm not exactly sure how to handle him. Pulling in a deep breath, studying his face closely, I narrow my eyes and cross my arms. Time to lay out the facts. I'm tired of this insanity.

"Whether you like it or not, Rocco, I'm a married woman." I lift my hand and wave the diamond and ruby ring on my left finger back and forth.

"You were supposed to be mine," he says, voice dropping, eyes narrowing in on the ring.

"But I'm not. And I never will be. Nor will Gia be yours either."

"I don't want Gia!" he screams and I take another startled step back, not expecting him to blow up so completely. My hands protectively drop again, lightly cradling my belly which immediately draws his attention downward. He takes a step closer, eyes turning into angry, little slits. "Are you carrying his baby?"

A strange look crosses his face and I take another step back, trying to keep as much space between us as possible.

"No," I instantly respond.

"Really?" His voice is casual now and he arches a brow. "Because Rossi boldly stated in front of everyone that you were probably carrying his child already."

"Well, I'm not."

"How can you be so sure? Weren't you at the doctor's office?"

"Yes, but it was just a routine physical." I do my best to sound casual, but I don't think he's buying it.

Rocco nods, clasps his hands behind his back and moves another step forward, effectively blocking me in the corner. "You know, Alessia, it really doesn't make a difference to me. Because here's what's going to happen. You and I were supposed to be together and I wasn't counting on Rossi to pull such a fucked-up stunt. I'm not going to pretend I'm not pissed that he had your virgin blood, but I'm going to look at the bright side. He broke you in for me and now I'm going to take full advantage. I'll be the one to put a babe in your belly and, if you're lying to me and there's one already in there, don't worry. It won't be for long. I'll have it taken care of and no one will ever know."

My heart drops sickeningly. Rocco has lost his mind if he thinks I'm leaving Miceli for him. And, there's no way he's going to harm my child. "You're talking crazy, Rocco. I'm married to—"

"No! Consider yourself a widow, my sweet. My men are hunting Rossi down as we speak and they'll take care of him for good. Just like they took care of Amato. Then I can finally take over running this city and strongarm the other families into listening to me."

My back hits the wall and I shake my head. "You're delusional."

"No, this isn't delusional. Delusional was when you told me you couldn't marry me after our first meeting."

"What're you talking about?" I ask, confused.

"Your insult pushed me over the edge a little and I may or may not have put a hit out on you." My jaw drops at his confession and he gives me the most dazzling, psychotic smile I've ever seen. "You must forgive me, my sweet. I was upset after your rejection and made a quick, reckless decision based on emotion."

"He *was* after me," I breathe. Miceli was right, but I never thought Rocco was the one who ordered the hit. A hit on me! Un-freaking-believable!

"But, he missed and everything turned out for the best, right? Now we can finally be together."

"He didn't miss! Miceli stepped in and protected me. If it wasn't for him, I would be dead right now."

Rocco shakes his head. "No, that's not what happened," he insists, eyes narrowing. "We were always meant to be. Rossi tried to stop that and now he's being dealt with. Everyone wants us to be together, even your parents." Then he lifts his arms, caging me in, and suddenly I'm trapped. He leans his head in far too close and I can smell his rancid breath. Pressing my lips together, trying to put more distance between us, I drop down and slide under his arm, but he reaches out and grabs me. His fingers dig into my flesh and I tug, trying to break free.

"Where do you think you're going, my sweet Alessia?"

"Let me go!" I yank hard, but his steel grip won't break. I'm starting to get scared and he's much stronger than I anticipated. He might not be nearly as muscled or tall as Miceli, but it doesn't seem to matter. His hold is unbreakable. And his eyes are utterly wild. "Please. You're hurting me."

Instead of loosening his grip, he yanks me right up against his body and plants his lips on mine. His kiss is hard and punishing, and my legs give out, knees buckling. Our mouths break apart and I gasp for air, trying to wipe his foul taste from my mind.

"Stand up," he hisses, "and kiss your soon-to-be-husband properly."

"No!" I cry and shove a hand against his chest. "You're not my husband! I am Mrs. Miceli Rossi and I will never be yours. Now let me go and—"

Rocco abruptly releases my arm and I stumble. Rage fills his light brown eyes and his hands clench into fists. "You are mine," he snarls. "And the sooner you accept that fact, the better off your life is going to be."

"Is that what you told Mercedes right before you killed her?" The moment the words leave my mouth, I know that I went too far. Rocco moves faster than a coiled snake, springing forward and backhanding me so hard, my entire face snaps sideways from the impact.

"Unless you want to end up just like her, I suggest you learn some respect. I will not tolerate a smart mouth on my wife." He clears his throat and runs his hands over his thighs, smoothing his pants. "I'm sure we can put that mouth of yours to much better use."

I'm still seeing stars when he reaches for my arm, guiding me out of the office. Even though his touch leaves me cold, I don't pull away because I'm too scared he's going to hit me again. Or worse.

"Now, let's get you settled upstairs."

The house is so big and I try to remember the layout as we walk through it. But, it's a lot to map out in my head and keep straight. Even so, I start counting doors, turns and hallways, committing them all to memory.

"This is your home now," he murmurs, "and I want you to be comfortable and feel secure. No one is going to take you away from me, my sweet. We are meant to be together. Once you accept your fate, your life will be much easier. Do you understand?"

Even though I nod my head and try to play it off like I've given up resisting him, that couldn't be any further from the truth. Because I'm going to fight Rocco Bianche off until the bitter end.

Until either Miceli comes to my rescue or…until my very last breath.

20

MICELI

The drive out to the Bianche estate seems to take forever and by the time we finally reach it, I'm on the verge of losing my mind. Every emotion is assaulting me, threatening to tear me apart or push me straight over the edge of sanity. Because if anything happened to Alessia, I'm going to lose my shit.

Vin pulls up along the rear of the property just as my inside pocket starts vibrating. I reach inside for Alessia's phone, pulling it out and checking the caller ID. She dropped it outside of the doctor's office when Leo was shot and one of my men found it and brought it to me. Now, I swipe my finger across the screen and answer.

"Hello?"

"This is Dr. Durant and I'm calling about Alessia Rossi's next appointment. Is she available?"

Next appointment? With a frown, my hand clutches the phone tighter. "This is Mr. Rossi. My wife isn't here right now, but—"

"Ah, congratulations, Mr. Rossi. You're going to make an excellent father."

Father? My heart stutters within my chest. "Ah, thank you," I say, playing it off like I already knew. But, inside my world is spinning as I try to wrap my head around the idea.

"Well, I'm just calling to confirm Alessia's next appointment and wanted to let you know that I have no problem making it a house call, per her request."

My throat tightens with emotion. "Thank you. I'll let her know." I have to choke out those final words and after I hang up, I stare down at Alessia's phone and feel something I haven't felt since I was a boy. The threatening sting of tears.

"What's going on?" Enzo asks from the back seat.

"Who was that?" Vin glances over at me from the driver's seat and, for a moment, I can't answer. Hell, I can barely breathe, much less form words. It feels like my throat is swollen and I have to force myself to speak.

"Alessia is pregnant," I tell them. My voice is flat and a fear more powerful than I've ever known before fills me. It's not just her life on the line anymore. Now an innocent baby is involved. *Our baby.*

"Oh, shit," Vin says.

"Pregnant?" Angelo echoes from the backseat.

Getting control over my emotions once again, I nod. "We can't let anything happen to her. Or, my baby. *Our* baby," I correct myself. *Holy hell—our baby. Alessia and I are having a baby!*

"We won't," Enzo states firmly. "Don't worry, Miceli. We're going to get her away from Bianche."

"Holy shit!" Angelo exclaims. "I'm going to be an uncle."

And I'm going to be a father. It's such a powerful thought and knowing I'm going to be in charge of that little life makes my heart swell.

"We're all going to be uncles. Not just you, dummy," Vin states.

"Yeah, but I'm going to be the fun uncle," Angelo announces.

"Of course you will be," Enzo says dryly. "You'll be the one to get the poor kid into all sorts of trouble."

"You bet I will," Angelo says, completely unapologetic.

I can't help but chuckle. My life is going to change in so many ways. Alessia has brought so much joy to my days. Days that used to be long and full of too much work. She's taught me how to relax and play. How to loosen my tie, slip out of my suit jacket and realize there is more to life than running an empire.

Alessia has shown me what it feels like to love. And I love her and our unborn baby fiercely. So damn much that I refuse to let anything bad happen to them. The more I think about Rocco and what he's done, the more angry I become. How fucking dare he take what belongs to me.

"Okay, we're here," Vin states. "Is everybody ready to do this?"

"I was born fucking ready." Enzo smirks arrogantly.

The idea of Alessia being in that house, locked up with Bianche who could have done absolutely anything to her by now makes me livid. A red haze settles over my vision and I practically throw the car door off its hinges when I open it. I yank my gun out and feel invisible smoke pouring from my ears. The urge to torture and kill Bianche leaves me feeling a little unhinged, and my brothers must see that because they're watching me closely. Vin lays a hand on my arm, halting me.

"Get it together, Miceli. Now isn't the time to lose your shit."

"I'm going to kill him," I growl.

"Take it easy," Enzo warns. "Otherwise, your ass is staying out here in the car."

"Like hell it is," I grit out, pulling free from Vin's grip.

"Going on a bloody rampage is only going to put Alessia in further danger. Lock it down." My gaze meets Vin's and I know he has a valid point. He's always been the wisest of the four of us. Five, if you count Carlotta, too.

After they talk me down, I pull in a deep breath and force a nod. "Let's do this," I say, keeping my expression neutral and my voice deceptively calm. We all walk over to the corner of the yard where we're going to scale the fence. The plan is simple: access the yard, sneak past the guards and find Alessia. Of course, that's the plan in its absolute basic, most simplistic terms.

Thanks to Archer, we now have a map of the mansion and since none of us have ever been invited over for a beer—shocker—these floor plans are priceless. Especially since the place is five stories with over fifty rooms to search. We've already determined that Alessia is most likely on the third floor—in the master suite. It pains me to admit it, but knowing what kind of scum Rocco is, it's the first place we're going to look. Even though I hope I'm wrong and she's somewhere else, I'm going to listen to my gut: he has her tucked away in his bedroom.

"Wait for the camera," Enzo reminds us, and we all watch, waiting until it moves and we're momentarily in the clear.

"Up and over," Angelo says, reaching for the wrought-iron bars. We all start climbing fast, keeping eyes on the nearby security camera, then round over the top of the spears and drop down on the soft grass below. Just as the camera begins to sweep back in our direction, we each duck out of sight behind a tree. We have a huge advantage because there are so many trees to use for cover as we make our way across the yard and up to the house. It's a mini forest back here and I send up a silent prayer of thanks. Because right now, we need all the help we can get.

Dodging from tree to tree, getting closer and closer, we keep a lookout for guards and cameras. As soon as we reach the perimeter of the woods, we pause and take a moment to study the situation. Vin silently motions to the right and I look over to see a guard walking along the back of the house. There are several more cameras and we're going to have to time this perfectly or get caught bringing the guard down.

Waiting, heart thundering in my ears, I time our attack on the guard along with the sweeping camera. Lifting my hand, I tick down the final seconds with my fingers, making sure the four of us are all on the same page.

Three...

Two...

One...

We burst out of the treeline and the surprised guard barely has time to react before I tackle him down hard. Enzo wraps a thick forearm around the man's neck and squeezes until he passes out. My younger brother is more than just a businessman and he's taken martial arts for years. If there's a way to bring a man down quietly, he knows the maneuver. And that's exactly what we need right now because we're relying on stealth to get this job done. Without a second thought, I slit the guard's throat.

Enzo and I drag the dead guard into the shadows of the large trees, making sure he's out of sight. Meanwhile, Vin and Angelo are working the nearest window up with some kind of fancy tool. It's small, compact and I'll have to remember to ask Angelo where he got that toy. Knowing Ang, he probably slept with some hot CIA agent. No one gets around like my youngest brother but, God love him, he's getting me into this house and that's what I need right now.

Enzo and I hurry over, making sure to dodge the camera, and meet Vin and Angelo who have the window up now. We each climb through and, once I'm inside, I look around the dark room, letting my eyes adjust. According to the map Archer sent, we should be in the music room. When I spot a piano, I know that's accurate. My heart does a funny, little lurch because listening to Alessia play for me every night these past few weeks has been one of my greatest joys. I've treasured every moment, every song, every melody that she's played for me.

She's going to play for me again, I vow. I'll make sure of it.

Quietly stalking forward, I reach the closed door and listen for a moment. Since I don't hear anything, I pull it open a crack and peer out. The hallway is deserted, but when I look to the right, I see the staircase we need that will take us straight up to the third floor. Then all we have to do is get down to Enzo's master bedroom.

And I hope that's where Alessia is. Otherwise, we have a damn big house to search and time is running out fast.

21

ALESSIA

Once we reach Rocco's bedroom, he turns to me, eyeing me unhappily.

"Before we spend the night together, you're going to need to shower. I don't want any of Miceli's filth still on you when I'm fucking you."

There's no way I'm letting Rocco touch me, but I know it's important to choose my battles wisely. And annoying him right now would be stupid. Instead, I nod meekly and pretend like his slap broke me. Far from it, though. If anything, it made me more determined than ever to break out of this prison.

"You have fifteen minutes. When I return, I expect you to be in my bed, naked and with those sweet thighs spread. Understand?"

God, he makes me sick. Swallowing back a retort, I nod then slowly turn toward the bathroom while mentally cursing him to the deepest, most fiery part of hell.

"Oh, and Alessia?"

I freeze and reluctantly glance over my shoulder.

"Be a good girl," he warns me. "I'm trusting you to behave yourself, but if you do anything stupid, I will hurt you. And believe me when I say I will make you suffer in ways you've never even imagined."

His words chill me to my very core and a shiver skates down my spine. I have no doubt that Rocco is cruel enough to punish me in a variety of creative and degrading ways. Hating him with a passion, but not daring to utter a word, I hurry into the bathroom and shut the door behind me. My hand automatically drops to lock it, but there's no freaking lock. With a sigh of frustration, I realize I have exactly fifteen minutes to figure a way out of here before Rocco returns.

What am I going to do?

Pulse racing madly, I flip the shower on and hope Rocco believes I don't plan on causing any trouble. Then, I slowly pull the bathroom door back open and step into the bedroom. It's ridiculously large and over the top. Everything is trimmed with gold and when my gaze lands on the king-size bed, I feel sick. If Rocco thinks he's going to ever get me in that bed, he has another thing coming. No fucking way.

On silent feet, I hurry over to the nearest window and look out. I'm three stories up and there's nothing but a neatly-manicured lawn below me. Leaning forward, pressing my forehead to the glass, I check to the left and right, hoping to see a trellis or something I can use as a handhold so I can climb down. But, there's nothing.

Think, Alessia. There has to be a way out of here. Something else that doesn't involve me potentially plummeting to my death.

But then it hits me—maybe it's not so much a direct way out that I'm looking for. Maybe, I can take advantage of this house's sheer size. A place this big has to have a lot of hiding spots. If I can find one, a really good one, and hunker down for a bit then that will give me more time to figure out the best way to get out. Also, it gives Miceli time to find me.

Miceli. God, I hope he's alright. Rocco said he has men after Miceli and I hope they haven't been able to find him. For all I know, he's still at the hospital with his brother. Unless…

Unless that entire thing had been a diversion. Rocco is such a conniving sneak, I wouldn't put it past him to lure Miceli away from me so his men could then grab me. But then that also means Miceli probably walked straight into a trap. I squeeze my eyes shut and pray he's okay. If anything happens to the man I love, I will lose it.

"Everything will be okay," I softly tell the baby. "It has to be because your dad is the most amazing man I've ever met. And he's going to love you so very much."

Pulling in a deep, resolute breath, I know what I have to do. After walking over to the door, I pull it open and look out into the empty hallway. Thank God—no one is in sight and it's quiet. Yanking it all the way open, I hurry out. I have no idea where I'm going, but when I reach the stairs, I start to go down then immediately hear voices. *Shit.* Spinning around, I silently race up instead.

My step is light and when I reach the fourth floor, I pause. Now what? Keep going up or hide somewhere on this floor? I'm grateful that this place is so big because it's going to take them a while to find me. Hopefully, they don't, but I have to be prepared that I might not find a way out.

If Rocco or his men catch me, I'm in big trouble. His earlier threat rings loud and clear in my ears, and I know he wasn't exaggerating. He will make me pay and he'll enjoy using pain and humiliation to do it. I can't believe my father ever planned for me to marry such a monster. What the hell was he thinking? And then to offer Gia over to him like some kind of second-hand sacrifice? My blood boils at the thought.

After wandering down the hall and peering into several rooms, I turn a corner and randomly look into a room. It's a gym and there really isn't anywhere to hide…except for a tall cabinet in the corner. I think

I'm small enough to fit inside and it's not somewhere that screams hiding place.

Scurrying in, I jog over and open it. There is some equipment, but I can definitely squeeze inside. Pushing a jump rope aside, I step into the cabinet and pull the doors almost all the way shut. I leave just a crack so I can look out and see if anyone comes inside the room.

Do I feel secure? Not at all. But it's pretty good for a temporary hiding spot.

Or, at least, that's what I think until the light switches on, flooding the gym with bright, fluorescent lighting. *Oh, shit.*

"Oh, Alessia..." There's a sing-song tone to his voice and I cringe when I see Rocco.

"What do you think you're doing, my sweet?" He practically spits the endearment out and I cower back against the metal wall. I am so screwed. How did he know I was in here so quickly? What did I do wrong?

"Do you think I was stupid enough to trust you?" He chuckles, moving closer, and I glance around, looking for something, anything, to use as a weapon. "This house is filled with cameras, my sweet."

Ugh. I wish he'd stop calling me that. It makes my skin crawl every single time. My hand reaches for the jump rope, pulling it off its hook. I'm not sure what good it's going to do me, but I wrap it around my hand and wait.

The moment Rocco opens the cabinet, I thrust my hand forward, using the end of the jump rope to stab him in the chest. With an oomph, he takes an unsteady step back, stumbling in surprise. I don't wait around to see what happens. Instead, I take off, running around exercise equipment and heading straight for the exit, needing to put as much space between me and Rocco as possible.

Unfortunately, I run straight into one of his enforcers. He grabs me and no matter how hard I fight, I can't break free. Rocco moves up behind me and I try not to flinch when I see the hateful gleam in his eyes.

"Bring her back down to my room," Rocco orders, voice harsh and dripping with venom.

I've done it now, I think, briefly squeezing my eyes shut.

Five minutes later, I force back tears as two of Rocco's men tie me down to his enormous bed. They stretch my arms and legs wide, securing them tightly to the bed posts, and I try not to succumb to the humiliation of being spread eagle for all to see. At least my clothes are still on and I take comfort in that small fact. Plus, I'm wearing leggings, not a dress, so I take a small comfort in that fact.

"Leave us," Rocco snaps to the enforcers. Then he turns his full wrath on me. "Well, congratulations, Alessia. You've managed to break trust with me in less than five minutes. After I explicitly told you what would happen. Why didn't you heed my warning?"

I'm not sorry and I don't even bother pretending that I am. My anger at the situation bursts forth and I glare at him. "You can do whatever you want to me, but it won't change a thing. I love Miceli, not you!"

Rocco stalks over and stares down at me. "You'll learn to obey me, Alessia. Or, you'll be punished. And, trust me, I'll take great joy in hurting you."

Telling myself to be strong and not cower, I refuse to break his stare. Until he reaches down and runs a hand over my stomach. My reaction is instantaneous, fierce and completely gives my secret away. Trying to twist away from him, I scream, "Don't touch me!"

Rocco straightens back up. "I'm bringing my own doctor in to examine you. And let's hope you're not pregnant."

My heart falls and an icy chill sweeps through my veins, instantly freezing my blood. Oh, God, no. I can't let that happen, can't let them hurt my baby. Because I know, without a doubt, that Rocco will take great pleasure in destroying the child Miceli and I created. A child made from love. A love that Rocco will never have or receive.

"Rocco, please," I murmur. "Please, just let me go. I don't know why you think we should be together, but—"

"Because you're mine! And because Miceli Rossi is going to be dead soon. Maybe he already is, and there's nothing you can do about it," he adds nastily.

"Damn you," I hiss, my fingernails biting into my palms.

Rocco hovers over me. "Last warning—behave yourself. The doctor will be here shortly and we'll rid you of Miceli's child, if need be. Then, you're going to lay back and take your punishment. I have so many things planned, my sweet. Just you wait..." I try not to recoil as his hand trails along my jaw then downward. He cups my breast then squeezes so hard, I yelp.

"Please..." I murmur.

"Get used to pain. You're going to be in a lot of it soon." He pinches my nipple then laughs.

I don't think I've ever hated anyone as much as I hate Rocco Bianche at this moment. When he finally leaves, I sag further into the mattress and tell myself not to cry. I refuse to give up and I'm going to hold it together and figure a way out of here. I have to—for my baby's sake.

Figuring I have one last chance, I tug at my bindings, but they're extremely tight. Looking around for something I can use to help me escape, I begin to panic. There's nothing. My breathing turns into hard, fast pants and I know that if I can't figure out a way to escape then Rocco's threats are going to come true.

And that's not something I can live with.

There has to be a way…

I refuse to accept any other possibility other than escape. But, it's like the one sliver of a chance I had to get out of here is now gone and there's nothing left I can do.

Nothing except lie here and wait for confirmation of the most horrible fate I can imagine. A fate that takes my husband and baby away from me forever.

22

MICELI

As we sneak through the house, we're fortunate enough to only encounter three guards so far, and we easily neutralize them. The estate is well-guarded, but we're like wraiths, moving silently as one. By the time they notice us, it's already too late. And we're not taking any chances. First, we bring him down; then we slit his throat.

The problem is this house is too damn big and we're racing against the clock. At this point, I think the best thing we can do is split up. As if he can read my thoughts, Enzo turns his attention to me and speaks them out loud.

"We should split up."

I nod. "I'm heading up to the master suite on three."

"I can take the second floor," Enzo states.

"I'll check out four," Vin offers.

"I've got five then," Angelo says.

"Be careful and text the others if you find anything," Enzo tells us.

I'm grateful my brothers know how to step up and take charge. Because right now, I need that desperately. My head is spinning and peppered with fear and doubts. I need to find Alessia before Rocco hurts her.

We start to climb the staircase and, halfway up, we run straight into a guard. His eyes widen in shock, but he recovers faster than I anticipate. Before we can reach him, he pulls his gun and fires. *Fuck.* So much for a quiet sweep and rescue. Going into survival mode, I yank my gun out and shoot back. The bullet hits him in the chest and he goes flying backwards.

"Go!" I urge my brothers up the steps. "Fast!"

We hustle up the steps, but stick to the plan and begin separating. Enzo rushes off on the second floor and then I break off on three.

"If you need backup, let me know," Vin offers.

"Okay, thanks." I'm waiting for chaos to ensue after those two gunshots were fired and it takes a minute, but agitated voices begin to echo up from below. Rocco and his men are about to find out they've been infiltrated. I need to find Alessia fast and I jog down the hallway, heading straight for the master bedroom.

Just before I reach it, three guards appear at the opposite end of the hall and I can see Rocco behind them. They raise their guns, but Rocco orders them to hold their fire.

"I should've known you were the one causing all this chaos," Rocco says.

"I haven't even begun yet, Bianche. When I'm through here there won't be anything left except a burning hole in the ground." I aim my gun at the group of men. "Where is she? Where's my wife?"

"She was never meant to be your anything, Rossi. She's mine. Always has been."

"You're delusional and I'm taking her out of here." I sidestep toward the master bedroom, taking a quick look inside, but I can only see the sitting room. "Alessia!" I yell.

"Miceli!" Alessia immediately calls back. I can hear the relief in her voice. "I'm in the bedroom!"

"I'm here, baby. Come to me."

"I can't. I'm tied to the bed!"

A rage fills me and I'm going to enjoy killing Rocco. Slowly and painfully. How dare he steal my wife and put her through this hell. Stepping into the doorway, using it as cover, I fire off a shot followed by another. The guards dive out of the way and Rocco disappears into a bedroom. I slip into the suite and slam the door shut. I hit the flimsy lock then drag a chair and lodge it beneath the door handle. Hurrying across the sitting room, I fire a text off to my brothers—*A on 3*.

Alessia on three. They'll know to come down and have my back.

Meanwhile, I burst into the bedroom, my attention moving straight to the bed where Alessia is tied up, spread eagle. "Alessia!" I race over and she looks up at me with those beautiful blue-green eyes.

"Oh, thank God, Miceli!" Tears fill her eyes and I do my best to suppress the rage threatening to blow.

Rocco isn't just going to pay for this; he's going to suffer first.

I immediately lay my gun down and start untying the rope securing her small wrist to the headboard. I'm so fucking angry, I can barely see straight. My hands shake and it takes me a minute to unravel the bond. "Are you okay?" I ask, checking out her chafed skin.

"I am now. I'm just so glad you're here and you're okay."

"I'm fine," I assure her.

"Rocco said he had men out looking for you. Hunting you down." A visible shiver moves through her small frame.

"I'm good and I'm getting you out of here," I promise. "Just hang on a little bit longer for me, okay?"

My wife nods bravely and my chest constricts. But, the moment the words are out of my mouth, I hear gunfire erupt in the hallway. Hurrying down to her ankle, I quickly start working on the rope when, out of nowhere, another gun fires. But this one is much closer.

With a curse, I realize the pillow beside Alessia's head now has a bullet embedded in it and feathers float in the air. Spinning around, grabbing my gun off the bed and lifting it, I see Rocco standing there. There must be a connecting room, I realize, and he takes a step forward.

"I'll kill her before I let you have her," he threatens.

As much as I want to take this asshole out, I need to play this carefully. One wrong move on my part could be the difference between life and death. Alessia's and mine. Keeping my hand steady and my aim true, I let out a low breath as different scenarios and their possible outcomes play through my head.

And I know without a doubt that one of us isn't going to leave this room alive—either me or Rocco. There's no way around that fact.

Ignoring the sounds of the gun fight happening out in the hallway, I focus all of my attention on Rocco. "You're not going to get away with this," I tell him.

"Really? Because I think I have," Rocco states arrogantly. "There's nothing you can do. If you spill my blood, the wrath of the Five Families will descend so fast your head will spin, and you'll be blackballed."

"Same goes for you."

Rocco shakes his head. "No, because you, Rossi, are going to be the victim of an unfortunate accident. Just like my dear, darling Mercedes was. God rest her defiant soul."

From the corner of my eye, I can see Alessia working on her bonds, so I do my best to keep Rocco's attention on me. I need to keep him talking. Play to his enormous ego and let him believe that he actually has a snowball's chance in hell of carrying this ridiculously bold stunt off. Of defeating me and making Alessia his.

"You killed her, didn't you?" I prod, referring to his missing girlfriend.

He shrugs an unrepentant shoulder. "Let's just say she and I weren't seeing eye to eye. We had a fight and, really, what happened was her fault. She brought it on herself."

"How can she be blamed when you're the one who ended her life?"

"That wasn't my intention!" he yells, face turning crimson with anger. "That dumb bitch came after me with a knife and I had to defend myself. I knocked the blade from her hand and shoved her. Shoved her really fucking hard because she turned on me. Showed me her true colors."

"What happened?" I ask in a low voice, doing my best to keep him talking. Alessia just freed her other wrist and I am so damn proud of her. She only has one ankle left and I need to make sure Rocco remains distracted.

"When she fell, she hit the side of her head on a table. Knocked herself out."

I take a step sideways, moving away from the bed and keeping Rocco's eyes on me. "Knocked herself out?" I echo.

"There was blood everywhere. At first I thought she was dead. But, unfortunately, she was still breathing. So, I had to take care of it. Finish her off."

"What did you do with her body?"

His brown eyes light up. "It's long gone. She'll never be found."

It almost sounds like he's bragging and my gut curdles. Rocco Bianche is a disgusting human being and I can't wait to end him. But, I need to bide my time and let Alessia get that final leg free. I'm about to ask him another question when Rocco turns and looks straight at Alessia. When he sees her trying to untie the final rope, his face twists and he shoots in her direction.

"No!" I launch myself across the bed, grab her and roll us right off the edge of the mattress. There's enough slack in the rope that she can land on the floor, but her ankle is caught and up in the air. I fire my weapon at Rocco and manage to graze his upper arm. He lets out a horrific scream and I quickly look down to make sure Alessia is unharmed.

Thankfully, Rocco's aim is absolute shit. Reaching over, I quickly finish loosening the rope and Alessia pulls her foot free.

"Stay down," I warn her. Using the bed as cover, I crawl forward and peer around the corner, but Rocco is gone. Fucking coward ran off. Straightening up, I realize he must've gone out the way he came in—through the adjoining room. "Stay here."

As I stalk across the bedroom, Alessia calls after me. "Be careful!"

It's time to end this, I think, my gait determined, my mouth set in a grim line. Staying to the side of the open doorway, trying to make myself a smaller target, I walk into the next room just in time to see Rocco unlocking the door to the hallway. Without thinking twice, I fire my gun and a bullet lodges in his back, most likely shattering his spine. With another ungodly scream, Rocco slams forward then slowly sinks to the floor, leaving a bloody trail down the door.

Stalking over to him, I kick the gun away that he dropped. He's lying on his back, eyes wide in disbelief.

"You'd shoot a man in the back?" he rasps, glaring up at me.

"Don't worry. I'll shoot you in the front, too." With zero hesitation, I put a bullet in his skull. I don't want to drag out his death. All I want is to end this, get my brothers out of here and take the woman I love home and wrap her up in my arms. Make sure she's safe. Always.

Rocco's eyes are glassy, unstaring, and blood oozes from the bullet hole in the center of his forehead. Maybe I allowed his death to be too swift, but I was never one who took a perverse enjoyment out of torturing an individual.

The point is, he's finally dead. *Thank fuck.* Slowly, I lower my gun, relief pouring through me.

"Miceli!"

I hear Enzo on the other side of the door, calling my name and pounding on it, so I unlock it and throw it open. My brothers swarm inside, assuring me the rest of the guards have been dealt with.

"The house is clear," Vin states.

I nod. "Rocco is dead." My voice is flat and I don't feel any sense of triumph over taking his life. I'm just happy it's finally over. My brothers stare down at his body, but no one says a word.

"Miceli?" It's Alessia and I spin around to see her standing in the bedroom doorway, looking unsure and a little wobbly on her feet.

Hurrying over, I sweep her up off her feet and cradle her in my arms. "You were so brave," I coo, pressing a kiss to her lips. "So damn brave, my sweet girl."

Alessia's arms wrap around my neck and she's clinging to me for dear life. "I was so scared I'd never see you again," she says softly, burying her face in my chest. I can feel the hot wetness of her tears soaking my shirt.

"You're okay now. I promise."

"Take me home, Miceli. Please."

And that's exactly what I do.

23

ALESSIA

The entire ride home, I cling to Miceli, terrified that he'll disappear and I'm only dreaming. That I'll wake up and find myself still tied to that awful bed in that horrible place. But, Miceli doesn't go anywhere and his strong arms hold me close as he whispers reassuring words in my ear.

I'm beyond grateful to him and his brothers; I owe them my life and that of my unborn child.

By the time we reach the skyscraper on Billionaire's Row, I'm feeling much better. More secure and like my old self again. Sitting on Miceli's lap, all curled up against his warm body, calms me like nothing else. The steady rise and fall of his firm chest lulls me into a light sleep.

The SUV stops and my eyes pop open. For a few minutes, I listen as the brothers talk.

"Maybe we shouldn't have torched the house," Vin says.

"No, it's best to get rid of it," Enzo states. "I wasn't about to bury all those bodies."

"They don't deserve a burial," Miceli says, the deep sound of his voice making his chest rumble against my cheek.

"So, now what?" Angelo asks.

"Now I'm going to have to face the Five Families. But ask me if I give a fuck."

"Do you give a fuck?"

I hear the car door open and Miceli begins to slide out, his arms tightening around me. He pauses, saying, "No. But, I will cover for all of you. As far as anyone is concerned, I went in there and rescued my wife alone. I won't drag any of you into what is going to most likely turn into the shit show of the century."

"Appreciate it, bro, but I'll go down swinging right beside you."

"Yeah, me, too."

"Same. You shouldn't have to face them alone."

My respect for Miceli's brothers couldn't get any higher. I lift my head and give them a small smile. "Thank you," I whisper.

"Any time," Angelo says with a wink.

"Go take care of your wife," Vin says. "I'll find out what's going on with Leo and send you an update."

"Appreciate it."

"Yeah, we'll talk later," Enzo adds.

"Thank you," Miceli says and they all nod, and we watch as the SUV drives away.

"Leo is okay?"

Miceli nods. "The doctor said he pulled through the surgery with flying colors and he's expecting a full recovery. He's just going to need a quiet place to recuperate, a lot of rest and probably some therapy."

"Hmm…" An interesting plan begins to swirl through my head. Even though she didn't finish, Gia went to school to be a physical therapist. Chewing on my lower lip, I wonder if I can set something up that will be…oh, I don't know, be mutually beneficial for my sister and Leo Amato.

"What're you thinking?" Miceli asks, eyeing me curiously. "I see the wheels turning."

"Oh, nothing. Let me think it through a little more and I'll tell you later," I say mysteriously, and he cocks a brow.

"Don't make me tickle it out of you," he warns.

"You wouldn't dare."

"Try me."

I laugh softly. "I really like your brothers," I tell him, changing the subject. "You guys are an amazing team."

"Yeah, they don't get much better than that."

He's still holding me so tightly, and I lay a hand against his beloved face.

"You can put me down now," I whisper, but he shakes his head and presses a kiss to my head.

"Not on your life."

"Okay, I'm not going to argue with you about it. Because there's nowhere else on Earth I'd rather be." Burrowing deeper into his arms, I sigh in absolute contentment. The elevator zips us up to the apartment and when Miceli steps out, Piero races over.

"Is everything okay?" he asks, sounding more worried than I've ever heard. "How are you and Mrs. Rossi and Mr. Amato?"

"We're fine, Piero. And Leo is doing well now. Thank you."

"What can I do?"

"Go home," Miceli says. "Take a few days off."

"Are you sure?"

"Yeah, I'm sure."

"If you need me—"

"We're good. But, thank you."

I give Piero a small wave and smile, and then Miceli carries me down to our bedroom. He kicks the door shut, walks over to the bed and sits. I'm expecting him to let me go but, I swear, he hugs me tighter.

"Oh, Christ, sweet girl. If I had lost you—"

"You didn't," I interrupt, pulling back and looking up into his dark, emotion-filled eyes. "I'm right here and, I promise, I am not going anywhere."

He forces a nod, swallowing down the lump in his throat. "I can't seem to let you go."

"There's something you should know…" I whisper.

Miceli reels back, face screwing up in panic. "Did he touch you?"

"No, no he didn't." I lay a hand along his stubbled jaw, feeling the tension drain from his body. "This is good news—I'm pregnant."

His mouth curves up. "I know."

"What? How do you know?" I ask, completely bewildered.

"Dr. Durant called your phone and I answered. He congratulated me."

My mouth drops open. "Ohh." I search his dark gaze. "Are you happy?"

He shakes his head and my heart sinks. "Not happy. I'm thrilled."

I release a breath and hug him tightly. "I love you, Miceli," I whisper, hugging him tighter, needing to be as close as possible to him.

He pulls back and stares at me. I could swear, there are stars in his eyes. "Say it again."

"I love you, Miceli Rossi. With my whole heart."

"Oh, God," he murmurs, burying his face in my hair. "I love you, too, Alessia. So damn much."

"Will you show me?"

I feel him nod, voice hoarse as he whispers, "Every damn day for the rest of your life."

"Take me to bed, husband."

Miceli pulls back and grins. "You never need to tell me twice, wife."

After carefully setting me next to him on the bed, we strip out of our clothes. When our bodies come together, skin on skin, it's the best feeling in the world. Absolutely glorious. Even though he's being incredibly gentle, there's a desperate undertone in his kisses and touches. Same with me, though. Almost losing one another puts everything into perspective fast.

Miceli drags his head down, kissing a pathway down to my breasts, circling my nipple with his tongue then sucking the hardened bud until my toes curl. Whimpering, I arch up as he releases my nipple with a pop and continues his way downward. He stops and presses a gentle kiss against my stomach.

"Our baby," he murmurs reverently.

Then he continues a little further south and his mouth latches onto my pussy. It doesn't take long before I'm a panting, crying mess. "Miceli, please," I beg. "I need you inside of me."

Crawling back up my body, Miceli settles between my legs and begins to slide his big, thick cock inside my soaked channel. I cry out, wrapping my legs around his waist, and try to pull him deeper. Desperately needing to feel every last inch of him buried inside of me to the hilt.

"Easy, sweet girl." He adjusts my hips and sinks all the way. We both gasp and, for a long moment, neither of us moves. We just relish the feel of being one. Then Miceli lets out a groan and begins to rock his hips. And, it's pure, undiluted heaven.

My nails graze down his smooth, flexing back and I lift my hips to meet each of his long, deep thrusts. It doesn't take long and the pleasure hits hard and fast. My inner walls squeeze tightly, contracting around his pulsing cock, and then Miceli explodes within me. We both moan through the euphoria and when he drops down on top of me, my arms hug him hard.

I'm never letting this man go. He is my everything and I will spend the rest of my life loving him. And I can't imagine a better future.

A little later, after we make love again, I'm snuggled in the crook of Miceli's arm and more content than I've ever felt in my entire life. Although, there is a part of me that's still worried.

"Miceli…"

"Hmmm."

I've never heard him sound so satisfied. "I'm worried about what's going to happen to you when the other Families find out what happened."

"I don't want you to worry about that."

"I can't help it. This is all because of me."

"No, it's not." He tilts my face up, meeting my gaze. "It's because of Rocco."

"Has this ever happened before?" I ask, my voice barely a whisper.

"You mean one of the five spilling another's blood?"

I nod.

"Not since the truce."

"What do you think they'll do?"

He sighs, lifting a strand of my hair and rubbing it between his thumb and forefinger. "I honestly don't know. Probably punish me somehow. Possibly even banish the Rossi family from the table."

I gasp. "But, that isn't fair."

"Nothing in this world is fair, sweet girl."

I push back, laying a hand against his chest, and frown. "Let's go talk to my father in the morning. I'm going to make sure you have a strong ally in him when you have to face the other Families' judgment."

Miceli nods. "Have I told you how very much I love you, Alessia Rossi?"

My mouth edges up. "Not in the past five minutes," I tease.

He grabs me, rolling me over and kissing me thoroughly. When he finally lifts his head, I look up into his beautiful brown eyes and see so much love. "Then let me say it again. I love you, I love you, I love you."

I start giggling then pull him down for another very long, very passionate kiss.

When morning arrives, we take a long shower together, get sidetracked, then finally get dressed and leave for my parents' house. It's Sunday morning and there isn't much traffic, so we make good timing. I already called and spoke to my mother, telling her we were on the way. I'm going to need her support now more than ever.

My mom welcomes me with a big hug and tells us she has pastries and coffee in the dining room. We follow her in and my father is already in there, drinking his caffeine and reading the newspaper.

"Hi, Dad." I walk over and kiss his cheek. "We need to talk to you. It's important."

He arches a dark brow. "What's going on now? Did you hear about the Bianche estate burning down? They can't find Rocco and think he died in the fire."

I exchange a look with Miceli. "We know, Dad, because we were there when it happened."

He sets the paper aside. "What're you talking about?"

"Rocco sent men to shoot Leo while he was guarding Alessia and then had her kidnapped," Miceli tells him and my mom gasps. "He was going to hurt her and kill me. But, my brothers and I stopped him. We took care of the situation and rescued Alessia."

Miceli doesn't elaborate, but his meaning is clear.

"It's true," I add softly. "I was leaving the doctor's office and Rocco's men grabbed me and shot poor Leo three times."

Another gasp fills the air and we all turn to see Gia standing there, her hand over her heart.

"Leo was shot?" My sister looks stricken by the news.

I nod. "He's going to be okay, though, Gia." She looks more than a little shell-shocked, but then slightly relieved when she hears he's going to pull through. I'm going to have to talk to her about my crazy plan. Because the more I think about it, the more I believe that she and Leo would make an amazing couple. They're exactly what the other needs and I'm going to do my best to play matchmaker, I decide.

"Doctor?" my mom echoes. "Is everything okay, Alessia?"

I give a little nod, suddenly feeling shy. "Um, yes." I look shyly from my mom to my dad. "Congratulations, you're going to be grandparents."

After a moment of surprise, they both smile and my mom claps her hands. Even Gia is grinning now.

"I'm going to be an aunt?" she exclaims, face lighting up.

I give her a bright smile. "Yes. But, only because Miceli and his brothers rescued me. Rocco said…" My voice trails off. "Well, he told me he was going to take care of Miceli's baby. Then he planned on forcing me to marry him."

"Oh, sweetheart." My mother walks over and hugs me. "That must've been so awful."

"It was but, thank God, they came. They saved me and our baby." I send Miceli a grateful look filled with love and he wraps an arm around my waist, pulling me closer.

"So you had to eliminate Rocco to save my daughter and unborn grandchild," my dad states. Miceli nods and then my father stands up and, for the first time, extends his hand to Miceli. "Thank you."

His voice is full of sincerity, and Miceli reaches out and they shake fiercely for an emotional moment.

"But, now we're worried about the other Families," I say, wringing my hands. "Technically, Miceli broke the truce, but he doesn't deserve to be punished."

"No, he doesn't," my father states, immediately supporting us. "What else can you tell me? We're going to build a solid case and present it to the table. I'll make sure we paint Rocco as the villain, and you, Miceli, as the hero."

My heart fills with relief and hope. For the first time, my family accepts my marriage with Miceli and now we're going to do everything in our power to make sure he comes out unscathed and on top.

Exactly where my husband, my hero, deserves to be.

24

MICELI

Although there are no clear rules, there has always been a mutual understanding that mafia blood of the ruling families shouldn't be spilled by each other. It's been three days since my brothers and I broke into the Bianche estate, I shot and killed Rocco and we burned all the evidence to the ground. Plus, we killed all of his guards and enforcers.

Do I feel bad or have regrets? No. I did what I had to do to save Alessia and I'd do it all over again without an ounce of hesitation. She's my world, my everything. No matter what, I will always keep her safe.

As a result of my actions, I've been summoned to the table for questioning by the other families. I knew it would happen and I didn't try to hide the fact that it was me behind the massacre at the Bianche estate. But, I did cover for my brothers because I don't want them dragged into the chaotic politics of the Families. The good thing is Aldo DeLuca is on my side and I need as much support as I can get. The bad news is that it still leaves three other powerful families that I need to convince of my innocence and of any wrongdoing. I don't plan on lying, though. I think the truth is the best option for me at this point.

I hope like hell that I'm right. Otherwise, this is going to be a damn short meeting.

My nerves are on edge and I know this could—and most likely will—end very badly. However, I feel good about keeping my brothers out of it. I refuse to drag them down with me. Alessia is my wife, my responsibility, and I will shoulder the blame for what I did. I've never considered myself overly honorable, but I'll keep my head up and say what needs to be said. I won't let this group intimidate me. I'm hoping with DeLuca as an ally, we can talk my way out of the mess that Rocco made.

When we reach the meeting place—we always try to arrange our meetings at a new location every time to avoid others from knowing —my palms are sweating. Alessia stuffed some hard candies into my pocket before I left and I find myself reaching for one. I unwrap the fruity candy and pop it in my mouth. She told me sucking on candies helps calm her nerves and I have no idea if it will help me, too, but, at this point, I've got nothing to lose. Plus, it makes me feel closer to her.

Today, we're meeting in an abandoned warehouse in the Meat District. The whole place has a rundown, ominous feel to it and I notice it's heavily-guarded on the outside. I walk past several very large, armed men, and finally I reach the door. I can feel their eyes on me, but I don't need to identify myself—everyone knows who I am. Even so, I find myself about to pull my credentials or some form of ID right before the lead guard waves me inside.

Get it together, Miceli, I scold myself, straightening up to my full height and snapping my perfectly-pressed suit jacket. You're not some wannabe thug sneaking into the big meeting. You're the head of the fucking Rossi family, arguably the most powerful clan in New York City. I deserve to be here and my family has earned its place among the Five Families.

Now, all I have to do is convince the people in this room not to kick me to the curb. I'm going to have to strike a fine balance because I don't want to come off like an arrogant prick but, at the same time, I've earned my spot. I've worked harder than anyone else here. Blood, sweat and tears built the foundation of my family's businesses and I worked my ass off to keep them growing and succeeding. I never shied away from the hard work needed to achieve the level of success I've found and maintained.

No one had better challenge or question my right to be here because of this damn incident with Rocco Bianche. But, of course, some bold fucker will and I'm going to need to strive for control and to keep it together. I'm going to need to defend myself calmly and not lose my temper.

Sometimes, that's easier said than done. Especially when I'm dealing with idiots.

I hate not knowing what's going to happen. And this is one time where I have no idea. Nothing like this has ever happened before and there's no previous, similar incident that we can look back on for guidance. Guess I'll be the one setting the precedent for all future situations where family turns on family.

Because, let's be realistic, it will happen again. With this much power and money, it's inevitable. I just need to hang onto my position at the table. And, I'm ready to fight tooth and nail to make that happen.

Pulling my shoulders back and putting on a steely expression, I step into the warehouse. It's dimly-lit and I'm expecting to see a large round table like always, so I'm surprised to see a long rectangular table instead. And a lone chair that faces the table. There are way more people here than I was anticipating. It's more than just the heads of the Five Families. There are also the second and third in line. Maybe I should have brought my brothers after all. A wave of nervousness sweeps through me, but I squash it down fast.

Swallowing down the lump of anxiety in my throat, I spot Aldo DeLucca and he gives me a slight nod. Not very reassuring, but I have to believe he's on my side. I just saved his youngest daughter's life. Of course, I also kidnapped her and forced her to marry me not very long ago after he rebuffed my proposal. But, I can't think too hard about that right now. *Focus on the positive, Miceli.*

Shit. Swiping a hand through my thick hair, I hope I can talk my way out of this and make the families understand why I did what I had to do. Because, truthfully, I wouldn't change a thing.

"Miceli, have a seat," Caparelli says, sweeping a hand toward the lone chair.

Here we go, I think, and walk over to the straight-back, wooden piece of furniture and sit down. It's uncomfortable, but I ignore that fact and sit up straight, ready to face the firing squad. That's what this whole thing feels like, anyway. I pull in a deep breath and face my possible executioners.

The other members of the families sit down at the long table and focus their full attention on me. I think the only thing we're missing is a spotlight on me. Though, it already feels like one is glaring down on me. Sweating bullets, I search for a friendly face and don't see one. *Fuck me.* This could get ugly fast. Especially when I see who is representing the Bianche family—Rocco's brother, Tommaso. He's just as unpredictable and dangerous as his brother was. Maybe even more so. And now his dark, rage-filled eyes are focused on me.

Caparelli begins the meeting with an explanation as to why we're all here and the longer he speaks, laying out every single one of my sins against the other four Families, the more defeated I feel. When he's finally done speaking, done fucking villifying me, I wish I could've brought a damn lawyer to defend myself.

Suddenly, my heart sinks down into my black shoes. I don't feel good about the situation and have a feeling I'm about to get my ass handed to me.

Gritting my jaw, I keep my head held high. *Bring it on, motherfuckers. Bring. It. On.*

"And so now it's our turn to act as judge and jury. As a group, we must determine if Rossi broke our alliance and what his fate will be. Let us begin the interrogation."

I guess since this whole situation has blown up into epic proportions, each family is allowed to choose three representatives to listen to my side, ask questions and then cast a vote that will decide my fate. Right now, I'm looking at three men and one woman, who are representing each family. That's twelve people I need to convince of my innocence. Not an easy thing to do. Especially when more than half of them look ready to shoot me down where I sit.

Everything is done in a very organized and efficient manner, as if we've done this before. Which, of course, we haven't. I get to be the guinea pig and face the table's wrath first. *Lucky me.*

The Milano family starts first and the questions begin. I get along alright with Old Man Milano, but his two kids...well, I don't know them very well and have no idea if they're going to give me a fair go of this or if they're going to crucify me to this wooden chair.

"Is it true that you were supposed to marry Gia DeLuca, but decided you'd rather have her sister?"

Ouch. Talk about cutting straight to the chase. This lovely question comes from one of Milano's sons and he's looking at me like I'm the devil incarnate. Whelp, all I can do is be honest. I truly believe it's my best option at this point. Besides, these people can smell bullshit a mile away. If I try to lie or pull a fast one, they'd catch on immediately. And then it would look like I was trying to insult their intelligence. *Can't do that.*

"I met both sisters and, while each was lovely in her own way, Alessia and I had an instant connection," I say honestly, remembering back to the first time we met in the DeLucca's library. I can't help but smile.

"There was something extremely special about her. I knew she was the one for me and I decided to pursue her."

"So then what? Because you had a so-called connection, you thought you could steal Rocco's intended and defy Aldo DeLuca's wishes?"

I lay my hands flat on my thighs and force myself to stay calm. I'm not going to get defensive. "I explained the situation to Aldo, but he wanted to keep things as they were—Rocco marrying Alessia and me marrying Gia," I say, trying to be as honest as possible. But, inside, I'm beginning to fume. I don't like the accusatory tone in this punk's voice. And, really? Who the hell can help who they fall in love with, anyway? Sometimes it's beyond our control. So, excuse me for wanting to marry the woman I love. I can feel my eyes narrowing slightly and I have to stop it and refocus.

Breathe, Miceli.

"So what did you do?"

I clear my throat, shifting in the hard seat. "I wanted to get to know Alessia better, so I followed her one evening, hoping we could talk. I needed to know if she felt the same way I did, if it was mutual. She took an Uber to Penn Station and told me she was running away because she didn't want to marry a man she didn't love. While we were on the sidewalk talking, a car screeched up and a gunman exited. He began firing at us, and I pulled Alessia down and killed the attacker."

"So someone tried to kill you and DeLuca's daughter was almost collateral damage?"

I shake my head. "No. Alessia DeLuca was the gunman's intended target."

Several people gasp and everyone starts whispering frantically. "How do you know that?" one of the Caparellis asks, voice full of doubt. "You're a much bigger threat than Alessia. The intended target was most likely you.

"No, it wasn't and I know this for a fact because Rocco admitted the truth. He told Alessia he was angry with her. Their conversation hadn't gone well and she told him she didn't want to marry him. In retaliation, he hired a thug to kill her."

Everyone starts talking at once and it takes a minute for them to quiet down. I was hoping that little tidbit of information would catch them all by surprise. Because Rocco Bianche was hardly innocent in all of this. In fact, he brought all of this on himself the moment he went after my woman.

May he rot in hell.

Once the table settles down again, Aldo DeLuca speaks up and, to my relief, he backs up what I've said and offers me his full support. This surprises several people and Milano instantly brings up my quickie marriage to Alessia.

"Didn't you steal her from her family and force her to marry you?"

"I didn't force her to do anything," I respond coolly. "I encouraged her to stay with me where it was safe and I could protect her better. I figured the best way to protect her was by giving her my name. After the vows were spoken, she said yes of her own accord."

The questioning goes on for more than an hour, but Aldo helps me reiterate one very important point—Rocco Bianche crossed the line first when he hired a hitman to take out Alessia. And that is unforgivable.

We also make sure they're very clear on the fact that Rocco kidnapped my pregnant wife, tied her up and threatened to hurt her and our baby. Everything I did from that point forward was to save Alessia and my unborn child. Yes, it resulted in Rocco's death, but by the time we reach this point in the story, I can see I have the table's support. Well, except for Tommaso Bianche and his two cousins, anyway.

But, am I surprised? Not at all.

After the questioning is over and I've said all I can possibly say to convince them of my innocence, Caparelli declares it's time to vote. I will either be blackballed from the Five Families or be forgiven. And, by me, I mean the entire Rossi family. We will all be punished because of what I've done.

And, let's face it. I did what I hope any of these other men would do in my position. I saved the woman I love. And I have zero regrets. Even if I get tossed out of here, I can go home and I still have the love of my life. There was a very scary moment when I could've lost her, but I didn't. And I wouldn't trade that outcome for a seat at the table.

I wouldn't trade Alessia for anything.

That's the last thing I say to them, too. I hope it resonates on some level because if I know anything about this group of people, it's that family is held in the highest regard. Blood is more important than our money and our businesses. Our family is everything, the very reason we do what we do.

This isn't a secret vote and, one by one, they go down the line and speak my fate. A simple "Yay" means I can stay on the table. A "Nay" means I should be blackballed.

There are twelve votes and I need ten to stay at the table. Holding my breath, I listen carefully as each man delivers his vote, sealing my fate. Hands clenched, trying to appear relaxed, I'm anything but calm. My hand twitches to pull out another hard candy, but I can't move. I'm frozen in place, listening anxiously as the votes are delivered.

"Yay."

"Yay."

"Yay."

Slowly, I release the breath I'm holding as a chorus of *yay's* fill the air. So far, so good. But, I need at least one of the Bianche's to vote yay. If all three vote nay then I'm out. And, I just killed their fucking family member. This isn't looking good.

Everyone votes in my favor and then it's time for Tommaso Bianche who is looking at me like he's willing me to drop dead. "Nay," he growls, lips twisting up in a sneer.

Can't say I'm surprised.

Tommaso sits with his two cousins, Romeo and Gabriella. Gabriella is the lone female at the table and she is never invited to meetings of the Five Families. She has a spark about her and she's attractive in a fierce kind of way, but she's also a loose cannon that is impossible to read.

"Nay," Romeo states, voice flat.

This is it. I meet Gabriella's caramel-colored eyes and prepare myself to be kicked off the table. She holds my gaze then folds her hands on the table. I can tell she likes sitting there and if I stay, I'm going to make sure she comes to more meetings.

If I stay...

"Yay," Gabriella says in a firm, steady voice.

I blink in shock. Yay? Did I hear her right? Rocco's brother starts yelling at her in Italian, so I know I must have heard her correctly. *Holy shit.*

"Congratulations, Miceli, the majority rules in your favor. You've been cleared of all charges and may remain at the table," Caparelli announces.

Feeling a little like I'm in a daze, I'm not sure what to do. Forcing myself up to my feet, I walk over to the end of the table and shake Caparelli's hand. I reach out to his other family and continue shaking everyone's hand, making my way down the line and saying a humble, "*Grazie.*"

By the time I reach the Bianche family, Tommaso has already stormed off, Romeo on his heels. But, Gabriella sits there looking as poised as ever.

"*Grazie*, Gabriella," I say and extend my hand. "You have no idea how grateful I am."

She shakes it, her grip firm, and grins at me. "The love you have for your wife is undeniable. It would be nice one day to have a man who loves me as fiercely as you do Alessia DeLuca. Excuse me, Alessia Rossi."

"I love her more than anything," I say sincerely, my chest tightening. "And I would do anything to keep her happy and safe."

"Clearly," she murmurs, then tosses me a mischievous wink. "Go home and tell her that, Miceli. Any woman would love to hear it."

My mouth edges up. Gabriella Bianche just got on my list of people I owe. Along with Archer. And, I vow I will repay her some day. I will repay both of them.

Now, however, it's time to go home and make love to my wife. Everything in the world is good again and I couldn't be more grateful.

25

EPILOGUE

ALESSIA

Eight Months Later...

Giving birth to our son was one of the most magical moments of my life. Right up until we welcomed our healthy, screaming eight-pound bundle of joy into the world, Miceli remained by my side. My entire pregnancy went relatively smoothly and I truly enjoyed the transformation my body, mind and heart went through. Now, however, I'm feeling the urge to get back into shape, but I think a few of the curves pregnancy added to my figure are here to stay. Miceli doesn't seem to mind, though, and he makes sure I know it.

Gliding back and forth in the rocking chair with baby Nico asleep in my arms, I sigh happily. I don't think I've ever felt this content or well-loved in my life. Being a mother agrees with me and it's a constant learning experience. Nico is now one-week old and he keeps us on our toes.

I run a finger over his chubby cheek and wonder how I ever got so lucky. Oh, wait, I guess it was the moment I walked into the library when I was supposed to go into the sitting room. One little misstep and the course of my life changed forever and in the most remarkable of ways. Because I found love. The kind of love that can only come from a good man who looks at me like I'm the most special woman in the world.

At least, in his world.

Miceli tells me every day, multiple times, how much he loves me. He also likes to remind me that the best thing that ever happened to him was finding me and then stealing me away. He doesn't agree that he forced me into marriage and prefers to say there may have been some coercion at first, but then I was completely onboard after that first kiss we shared in his bedroom.

He isn't wrong. That first kiss left my heart thundering, my stomach flipping and my knees quaking. It's funny because even now, his kisses still affect me that way. They make me just as giddy as they did that very first time.

When I see a shadow, I look up and speak of the devil. My big, handsome protector stands in the doorway, gazing softly at us.

"Hi," I murmur, a smile lifting the corners of my mouth. "How was your meeting?"

"Considering how power hungry that group of people is…I'd say it went extremely well." After the chaos revolving around Rocco, Miceli and his brothers decided it would be in the Five Families' best interest to create a solid alliance. Instead of only the family heads meeting, anyone from the family is welcome to attend their clandestine meetings and vote on decisions that need to be made. It helps spread out and better balance the power. Plus, by creating this Alliance, they're all working together to protect each other's best interests, rather than working against each other. So far, it's going well. But, some members of the Bianche family are still harboring a grudge and enjoy making things difficult. Miceli has to keep a close eye on them, but he assures me everything is running more smoothly than it ever has before.

Miceli strides over on silent feet, leans down and presses a kiss to my lips. And, yep, my stomach somersaults.

"Hello, princess. How's our little prince doing tonight?"

"Wonderful. No fussing at all. He just finished eating about ten minutes ago and fell right to sleep."

I watch as Miceli reaches for Nico's tiny hand and holds it. It makes my heart weep tears of joy.

"I don't think I'll ever get used to how little he is. Sometimes, I'm scared I'm going to break him."

"Never. You're too gentle. Enjoy it now though, Daddy, because your son is going to grow up to be big and strong one day. Maybe even bigger than you with the way he eats."

Miceli lets out a low chuckle, his dimple appearing. I love that dimple and the boyish look it gives his rugged face.

"He does have a healthy appetite." He releases the baby's tiny fist and caresses an index finger along the open edge of my robe where my absolutely huge breasts threaten to pop out. "Can't blame him, though."

"Naughty," I whisper.

"When did the doctor say we're allowed to…" His words fade away in a low grunt as he palms my breast.

"Miceli," I chastise. "You've got about six more weeks before that. I swear, you're insatiable."

"When it comes to you, yeah, I'm a hungry man, princess…starving…"

"Kiss your wife," I murmur, and he needs no further invitation. Miceli's hand moves back up to cradle my neck and he leans in, his lips capturing mine. I'll never tire of his kisses and my toes curl in my slippers. So deep, so thorough. I whimper softly in the back of my throat as his tongue slides against mine.

When we finally come up for air, his dark eyes look a little glazed over. Knowing I have the power to bring this big, powerful man to his knees is heady.

"I've never been so damn happy," he says softly. "You're my everything, my sweet girl, and I'm going to spend the rest of my life showing you just how much I love you."

"I love you, Miceli." He reaches for my hand, lifts it to his lips and brushes a kiss along my knuckles. Then our fingers entwine as we gaze down at the little miracle in my arms. "Since it was just me and Gia, I always wanted a big family. Have I mentioned that?"

His dark brows shoot skyward then his mouth edges up. "Alessia, I promise to keep giving you babies until you say stop."

"What if I want ten?"

"Ten?" he echoes dubiously, but I keep my face serious and nod. "Then ten it is."

"And if I change my mind and decide I'd like fifteen?" I try not to laugh at the expression that crosses his face.

"You plan on keeping me very busy, don't you?"

I can't help but grin. "I'll take whatever you give us, Miceli. It doesn't matter if it's one baby or twenty."

"Twenty might be a little much, princess, but we have time."

"I think we have our hands full with Nico. For now, anyway." I toss him a playful wink. "But, when that six weeks is up, husband dear, you better be prepared to get busy."

"You know," he begins thoughtfully, "there are other things we could do until then."

"Oh?"

"Maybe if you put Nico in his crib, I'll take you to bed and show you a few things."

I chuckle and shake my head. "Insatiable."

"Only for you, my princess."

Miceli helps me up out of the rocking chair and we tuck Nico into his crib. Then, my husband guides me down to our bedroom and he shows me exactly how much fun we can still have despite the doctor's orders.

EXCERPT: CHARMED BY THE MAFIA

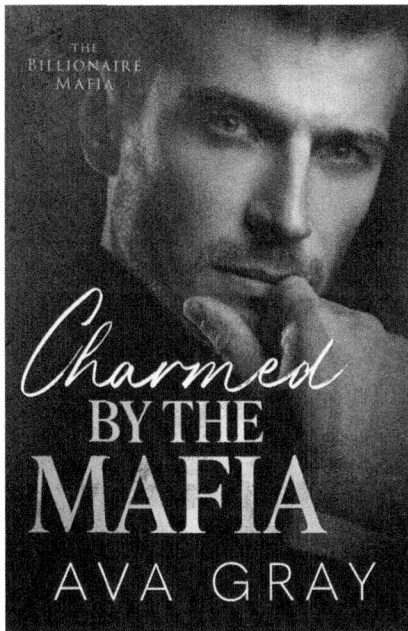

O nly a billionaire mafia could think he could escape death.

I'm his heart specialist, and he's the patient I absolutely can't resist.

So, when he called me his girlfriend to please his family, I could only nod in agreement.

Giovanni might be my forbidden patient and fake lover…

But I have real dreams about him taking my V-card.

Soon, these dreams would turn into nightmares.

His life is filled with danger.

And mine feels heavier now that I'm carrying the burden of his secrets.

Giovanni only has a few months left to live if we fail at treating him.

But I may not even have that much time remaining.

Giovanni will have to find a way to save my life from his own people.

Especially now that I'm carrying the child, he'd never want to lose…

Giovanni

Something isn't right.

The thought filters through my head as I struggle to pull in a breath. I'm halfway up the stairs and it feels like my heart is going to explode right out of my chest. After swiping a hand across my sweaty brow, I lay my palm against the wall above the railing and try not to panic.

For several moments, I don't move and just listen to the rapid drumming in my ears. Yeah, something is definitely wrong with me, and I have a feeling it's not good.

Lately, any little thing I do takes a herculean effort. And it's beginning to worry me. However, I've been doing my best to ignore the odd symptoms popping up. Like how my thirty-one-year-old ass can't walk up a flight of steps without getting winded. Or, how I'm always tired all the time no matter how much sleep I get. Which, of course, only makes me more grumpy than usual.

I keep telling myself I'm young and it's nothing serious. No need to worry. There's also the ridiculous amount of stress I'm under, too, and that would be enough to make anyone not feel well. My father is looking to me to take over the family business so he can retire soon. Matteo Marino knows how to apply the pressure and pour on the guilt to get his way.

Maybe any other eldest son would be excited and chomping at the bit to take over a billion-dollar empire. My father has certainly prepared me for it. But, lately, the honest to God truth is I don't want it. Any of it. Not the multi-million-dollar corporations, not the shady underground dealings and certainly not the weight of his legacy. It's suffocating.

Which probably wouldn't make sense to most people. But do I really want to be remembered like he will be? As a ruthless man who would choose money over his own family? A father who disinherited his daughters because they married rivals? A grandfather who chose not to meet his grandchildren because he couldn't come to terms with the fact that his daughters fell in love with men from the O'Shea family? Same with his son. My younger brother Luca recently wed Finley O'Shea. And what started out as a contract eventually turned into something real and beautiful.

The reality is my father's billion-dollar empire was built on selfish decisions, eliminating rivals and dirty dealings. The whole thing makes me a little sick. But he keeps looking at me, expecting me to be excited about stepping into his shoes. And I'm not. I haven't been feeling well for weeks now and, even though I'm trying not to worry about my deteriorating health, I can't help it. The symptoms are getting to be too much to ignore. Though I'm still trying my damndest to pretend like I'm healthy as a horse.

Even though I can't walk up a goddamn flight of stairs.

This is ridiculous, Gio. Get your shit together. You're fine.

I lay a hand on my chest and feel the rapid, out of control beating of my heart. Squeezing my eyes shut, I stand there and wait until it slows down and I'm breathing more normally again. Then I open my eyes again, look up the steps and realize I have about ten more to go.

But it may as well be one thousand. *Fuck.* I drop down on a step and rake my fingers through my thick, dark hair. What is wrong with me? Trying not to panic, I spend the next few minutes convincing myself I'm just under a lot of stress. Maybe I'm having a panic attack. I'll go to bed earlier tonight. Lay off the whiskey. Start taking my vitamins again. Everything will be fine and go back to normal.

Or, at least, that's what I try to convince myself.

"Get up, Gio," I growl under my breath. Reaching for the hand railing, I gather up my strength, and pull, heaving myself back up onto my feet. It takes some effort, but I stand up and nod. Okay, I did it. We're good to go.

I force myself to walk up the rest of the steps and, by the time I reach my bedroom, I'm ready to pass out from exhaustion. Dropping down onto my bed, I sprawl out on my back, a hand falling on my chest, and gaze up at the ceiling. I just need a quick nap. Then everything will be better after I'm refreshed and rested. My head turns to look at the clock on my nightstand. It's only eleven in the morning and I got up two hours ago. Yet, my body feels like it's been going nonstop for hours already. Days even.

Yeah, something is definitely not right, but I'll feel better after a nap. Twenty minutes ought to do the trick, I think, as I doze off.

Five hours later, the ringing of my phone wakes me up and I'm shocked to see how long I slept. I grab my phone, swipe the bar over, and try not to yawn, as I answer.

"Hey, Luca."

"Gio! I'm running late, but I'll be there in twenty minutes."

Late? For what? Pushing myself up onto my elbow, I frown.

"Sorry, but Finley and I were—" His voice trails off.

Yeah, I can pretty much guess what my younger brother and his pretty wife were doing. They're still newlyweds and even though the whole thing started out as an arranged marriage and they signed a contract with the intention of getting it annulled after three months, they fell in love. Hard and fast. Just another twisted thing my father set up to help himself. Although, he told all of us he regretted disinheriting Rory and Sofia and wanted to make up for it by fully supporting Luca and Finley O'Shea's marriage…of convenience.

But, once again, he was only lying to benefit himself.

"Yeah, I get it," I tell him, smothering a chuckle. "I'm, ah, actually running a little behind myself."

"Do you want to reschedule?"

"Nah, it's fine. I'll see you twenty."

"Okay, see you soon!"

After hanging up, it occurs to me yet again that Matteo Marino's ulterior motives always root back to his desire for more power and more money. As if the selfish bastard didn't have enough. He never cared about mending relations between our family and the O'Shea family like he claimed. He merely wanted to rally and build up support from his friends and business associates so they would turn on Desmond O'Shea who had taken over his family's business dealings.

But, after a war with Desmond, the O'Shea's triumphed, regained control of their compound and empire, and now Desmond is dead.

My father managed to put on a good show for a while and we all thought he turned over a new leaf. Yeah, right. Eventually, his true colors showed, and Luca told us he wasn't willing to trade Sean Flannigan, his captive, to save Finley's life. Flannigan was a pawn in his game and one he refused to give up. Even if it meant letting the woman Luca loved die.

Of course, Luca didn't allow it to happen, and he and the O'Shea brothers rescued Finley from Desmond's clutches. After a showdown on the upper level of their compound, Desmond somehow plummeted to his death. Finley was the only one with him when it happened, and it boggles my brain to think that tiny redhead managed to kill her evil uncle. I don't know all of the details, but, somehow, she took care of him, and it was a good thing.

Now, though, everyone is mad at my father again because he handed Finley over to the wolves. After escaping, she told us Desmond said he'd hired an assassin to take Matteo out. We aren't sure if that's true or not, but my father hasn't been leaving the house and I'm pretty sure he's beefed up the security. So, I'm going to assume he's worried about Desmond's threat. And I wouldn't put it past the man. He was out for everyone's blood, mostly his own family's, but he and my father hated each other.

Pushing thoughts of my father aside, I sit up, slide my legs off the bed and pause before standing up. Then I pull in a deep breath and stand up to my full height. Okay, so far, so good. No dizziness or exhaustion. Yet.

But I still have to change, drive over to the tennis courts and play a physical game against my very athletic, younger brother. I have a pretty good feeling that I'm going to suggest we end the game early and go down to the bar to get a drink instead.

Once I'm wearing sweatshirt and sweatpants, I grab my racket and coat and head downstairs. Even though it's a nice day, it's still the end of November in Chicago and that could mean anything. Sun one minute, rain the next.

Going down is easier than coming up, so I'm feeling pretty good. I head outside, jog down the steps of the brownstone—I never realized how many goddamn steps this place has until they started taking their toll—and slip into my Porsche Panamera parked at the curb. It's a super luxurious car while also being sporty and perfect for me because I enjoy having the best of both worlds.

The tennis courts aren't far away and, by the time I get there, get out and walk onto the court, I'm still feeling good. Relief washes through me. All I needed was a nap. Nothing to worry over.

Luca isn't here yet, so I gratefully drop onto a bench and set my racket down. Even though I'm feeling okay at the moment, I don't want to over-exert myself. Luca is competitive and so am I, so neither of us takes it easy on the other. We both like to win.

Draping an arm along the back of the bench, I look up at the trees. The few leaves that are left on the trees are barely hanging on, fluttering in the breeze. Just a few weeks ago, they were all different colors, so vibrant and pretty. I love the seasons and how the leaves change from green to orange, gold and red. I've never minded the cold weather and right now it feels invigorating. Refreshing and crisp as it fills my lungs, expanding them.

Slipping my coat off, feeling a little warm, I realize it's going to be December soon and then Christmas in the blink of an eye. The holidays seem to sneak up faster and faster every year. Things are so different now that my siblings are all married. Rory and Liam have a son named Griffin who is a year and a half, while Sofia and Rafferty have Killian. Luca and Finley just found out they're pregnant and I'll have a new nephew or niece next June. It's a little mind-boggling.

I'm happy for them and the love they've found. But the truth is I've been feeling a little lost. And a lot out of the loop lately. Now that my sisters and brother have found their significant others, I don't see them as much. They're busy with their families and I get that. My mom also moved out of the brownstone not long ago and is living over at the O'Shea compound. It seems that just about everyone has left. They've had enough of Matteo Marino and all of the hurt he's caused.

I'm not sure why I'm still there. But I think it has to do with the fact that I have nowhere else to go. No one needs me and that's a little depressing. A part of me would like to have a girlfriend, but that involves a lot of energy and work. And, let's face it, I can barely handle getting up the stairs.

There was a serious girlfriend a long time ago, but it didn't last. At the time, I think I loved her, but things didn't work out and we went our separate ways. It was hard at the time, but nothing I couldn't get over. I've never had trouble attracting women. I think they like the broody, not interested vibes I give off. But, for whatever reason, I lose interest fast and nothing lasts past a couple of dates and a romp or two in the sheets.

My siblings are lucky, but I'm not sure it'll ever happen for me. Love is a strange thing, and no woman has ever had the power to sweep into my world and knock me off my feet. Honestly, I doubt the perfect woman even exists for me. Hell, even if I could make her up from scratch myself, I don't even know what I want. Blonde? Brunette? Short? Tall? Bubbly? Smart? Funny? Silly?

Eh. Who knows? I sure don't, so it's really not a surprise that no one is able to catch my attention for long.

I glance down at my watch, wondering where my brother is, then look up right as Luca's Mercedes pulls up behind my car. It's about time. Unzipping the case that holds my racket, I pull it out and stand up. Luca walks over and we bump knuckles.

"Your wife is already knocked up," I tease him good naturedly. "Give her a break, Jesus."

Luca laughs. "Yeah, right. I can't stay away from her. It's like she's a drug and I just want to be high on her all the time."

"That's a lovely analogy," I say dryly.

"Hey, I never claimed to be a poet."

There's a warm glow in his brown eyes and it appeared after he met Finley. My younger brother can turn on the charm, but now he saves it all for his wife. I used to be able to be charming, but now I can't be bothered. It takes too much energy and there's no woman I've met lately that makes me want to exert that kind of effort. Especially, when I'm so damn tired all the time.

Relationships are hard work and I have way too much on my plate right now. Or, so I try to tell myself.

"C'mon, old man," he says and bounces a ball with his racket. "I'm ready to beat your ass."

"Yeah, right. Not gonna happen."

We move to opposite ends of the tennis court and Luca tosses the ball up and slams it hard. I run forward and hit it back over the net. We go back and forth for a little bit until I miss, and Luca whoops it up.

Trying to ignore the intense beating of my heart, the flutters I'm feeling at the hollow of my throat, I shake my head and lift my middle finger. Once I'm back in position, knees bent, I spin my racket and keep my eyes on the ball. Luca serves and I race forward and slam my racket into the ball, sending it right back over the net and barreling over where Luca easily hits it back.

Shit. I hurry to reach the ball, but miss, and suddenly it feels like a freight train is running over my chest. With a gasp, I drop my racket, lean over and plant my hands on my knees, wheezing. Trying to catch my breath is beyond me at this point and I hear Luca calling my name.

It's the last thing I hear, too, because suddenly my knees buckle and I drop to the ground, my head hitting the hard pavement.

Read the complete story HERE!

SUBSCRIBE TO MY MAILING LIST

I hope you enjoyed reading this book.

In case you would like to receive information on my latest releases, price promotions, and any special giveaways, then I would recommend you to subscribe to my mailing list.

You can do so now by using the subscription link below.

SUBSCRIBE TO AVA GRAY's MAILING LIST!

1023 6307681

Printed in Great Britain
by Amazon